In the remote village of

Aidan

Join Aidan and his friends, Lilly and McKenzie, as they embark upon the journey of a lifetime. Just before his thirteenth birthday, Aidan learns of a prophecy that holds the key to ending the terrible war.

Lilly

Aidan must leave his home to fulfill his destiny and bring peace to the land.

On this journey, Aidan and his friends learn the true meaning of courage, the importance of compassion, and the value of friendship.

McKenzie

Jacket Illustrations by Judith Friedman.
Jacket design by Judith Friedman.

Goth
ORROW SEA
Olsburg
Castledom
Stonebridge
Abyss of Charon
Rock of Algadon
Gilan Desert
Land's End
N
W
BOTHAM SEA

Aidan of Oren

The Journey Begins

Aidan of Oren
The Journey Begins

By Alan St. Jean
Illustrated by Judith Friedman

Published by Moo Press, Inc.
Warwick, NY

✦

Published by Moo Press, Inc. Warwick, NY. For information on permission to reproduce, or about this and other Moo Press titles, please email info@MooPress.com or write to Moo Press, Inc. PO Box 54 Warwick, NY 10990. To obtain copies of this book, visit your local bookstore or our website at www.MooPress.com.

Map of Lionsgate by
Megan D'Arienzo, Jr.
Text set in Adobe
Garamond.
Titles set in
Humana Serif.

Cover design and
illustrations by
Judith Friedman.
Illustrations
were rendered
in pen and ink with
watercolor for the cover.

PUBLISHER'S CATALOGING-IN-PUBLICATION DATA
St. Jean, Alan.
Aidan of Oren: the journey begins / by Alan St. Jean; illustrated by Judith Friedman.
— Warwick, NY : Moo Press, 2004.
Audience: ages 7-12.
Summary: Aidan learns that he is the hero of legends long told. As such, he must leave his hometown to find the elves who can teach him the skills needed to free the guardians and end the war that ravishes the countryside.
ISBN: 0-9724853-5-X
1. Responsibility—Juvenile fiction. 2. Interpersonal relations—Juvenile fiction. 3. Heroes—Juvenile fiction. 4. Adventure stories. 5. Fantasy fiction. 6.[Fantasy.] I. Friedman, Judith. II. Title.
PZ7.S34 A433 2004   2003111730
813.6—dc22   0411

Printed in the United States of America
BVG 10 9 8 7 6 5 4 3 2 1

"For Judy, the love of
my life. Thank you for
believing."
—Alan St. Jean

"For Jean-Pierre,
with all my love."
—Judith Friedman

TABLE OF CONTENTS

Aidan of Oren

CHAPTER 1

The Awakening

"AWAKE...AWAKE!" A voice broke the night silence. Aidan sat straight up in bed. He looked around his bedroom, but no one was there.

"Odd," he thought. "Was I dreaming? But it was so real."

He sat motionless, listening, hardly breathing. As he looked from shadow to shadow, his eyes pierced the darkness. All seemed in order. Slowly and silently, he pulled his quilt aside and stepped out of bed. The wood plank floor beneath his feet felt cold as he moved across the room. Perched in the corner was Aidan's pet falcon, Charles, fast asleep.

This was not the first time Aidan had been awakened by a dream. Lately he had been having many dreams...dreams about castles, knights in shining armor, ferocious dragons, giants, and curious elves. Ever since he was very little, Aidan was intrigued by the stories told by the old women of the village. They often gathered together in the fireplace room here at his Grandmama's cottage to work on quilts, and while they did, they told the most magical stories.

AIDAN'S BEDROOM WAS RIGHT BESIDE THE FIREPLACE ROOM

The Awakening

Aidan's bedroom was right beside the fireplace room. He looked forward to these nights...Grandmama would come into his room and tuck him into bed. With a gentle kiss on his forehead, she would whisper goodnight and return to her friends just outside his door.

After pretending to be asleep, Aidan would crawl out of bed and peek through a crack in his door. He would watch and listen—often late into the night—hanging on every word as the stories would unfold. The old women told tales of adventure; some funny, some scary. Grandmama was the very best storyteller of them all. But, they were just stories...stories told around the glowing warmth of a roaring fire.

Aidan moved toward the door and peeked through the crack into the fireplace room. The glowing embers revealed only that the room was now empty. The old women had already gone home. Still confused by what he had heard, Aidan went back to bed. He shuffled around on his hay-filled mattress and wrapped himself tightly in Grandmama's quilt. Finding a comfortable spot, he lay back and stared at the ceiling.

Although he was used to dreaming about the stories he overheard, tonight's dream was different. Tonight, Aidan had dreamed of a magnificent horse. But not just any horse—a pure white horse with wings. None of the stories told by his Grandmama or her friends mentioned such a horse.

Aidan of Oren

"AWAKE…AWAKE!" The words still echoed in his head. It all seemed so real, but it must have been a dream. What else could it be? Eventually, Aidan fell back to sleep.

CHAPTER 2

The Well

ood morning, Aidan," said Grandmama as she opened the shutters, flooding Aidan's bedroom with a burst of sunlight. "I trust you slept well?" she said with a twinkle in her eye. Aidan slowly sat up in bed, rubbing his eyes and nodding toward his grandmother.

"Breakfast will be ready soon. Would you fetch some water for me?"

"Of course, Grandmama," said Aidan. "I had a dream last night."

"That's nice, dear," she said as she moved toward the door to leave the room.

"It was about a beautiful white horse with wings!"

Grandmama stopped suddenly. "What did you say?"

"I was telling you about my dream," Aidan said excitedly. "I saw a great white horse with enormous wings flying through the air. It was dark. I was barefooted, and standing outside in the middle of the night."

Grandmama took a step back into Aidan's room. "If it was dark, how can you be sure that the horse you saw had wings?"

"That's the best part! He walked right up to me! The

17

moon was bright, and he was so close I could see every detail. He was the most magnificent beast I've ever seen."

"Was that all of the dream?" she asked.

"No, there was a voice. It was a very big voice, but it didn't come from the horse. It wasn't that loud, you know, but it was big."

"What did this voice say?"

"It said, 'Awake! Awake!'"

"I see," she said softly as she walked out of his room and started to close the door. "Thirteen years. My, that went by fast, didn't it, boy?"

Aidan wondered about Grandmama's odd remark. True, his thirteenth birthday was only two days away, but what did that have to do with his dream? He started to ask, but it was too late. Grandmama had already closed the door.

Aidan sat quietly on his bed. Facing the open window, with his eyes closed, he soaked in the morning sun and smiled broadly back at the light that seemed to wrap itself around him. The warmth felt good, and the gentle breeze whispered in his ears.

His thoughts turned back to Grandmama; she was the only parent that he had ever known. He could not imagine life without her. Long ago, Grandmama had told him that when he was a baby, his parents had brought him to the country of Lionsgate. They had placed him with her in a remote area just south of Oren Village, between the Botham Sea and Zorn Mountain. Something about a war—but it was only supposed to be for a while.

The Well

He · Smiled · to · Himself · as · He · Headed · Toward · the · Well ·

Aidan of Oren

Grandmama did not often speak of Aidan's parents. He knew only that his father was a very good man who was needed by people in a land far away. As for his mother, Grandmama spoke of her very warmly, as if she was love itself. Aidan longed for the day when they would be reunited.

Opening his eyes, Aidan could see that it was a clear morning. Somehow, it seemed brighter than an ordinary sunny day. He chuckled to himself as he quickly put on his clothes and headed out the door.

"Brighter than a normal sunny day," Aidan said aloud to himself. "Am I going crazy? A sunny day is a sunny day, and that is that. Maybe I didn't sleep so well after all." He smiled to himself as he headed toward the well.

As he walked around to the back of the cottage, he could feel his legs starting to tense. Aidan didn't like the well. It was very old, and very, very deep. The stones that surrounded it were ancient and cracked. The opening of the well wasn't even round. Rather, it was somewhat oval shaped, curiously larger at one end than the other. When he was younger, Aidan used to drop rocks into the well, listening for them to hit something— anything. However, he never heard a sound. Yet, every time the bucket was lowered into the well, it always came up with sparkling clean, fresh water. This was a mystery to Aidan; it even made him feel a little afraid. However, he told no one for fear that some might view him as cowardly.

The Well

Today, as he lowered the bucket and watched it disappear into darkness, he felt even more anxious than usual. Maybe it was because of last night's dream. Aidan focused on the task and tried very hard to ignore the butterflies in his stomach.

As he began to draw the bucket up from the well, the crank jammed. Startled, Aidan froze. The bucket was caught on some rocks about three feet from the top of the well. Aidan was petrified with the thought of reaching into the well. As he pondered his dilemma, two small hands reached around his head and covered his eyes.

"Guess who?" shouted a gleeful little voice.

Aidan was startled, but quickly recognized this game. He put his hands over the ones on his eyes and said teasingly, "Is it a baby bear?"

"No!" shouted the little voice, bursting into laughter.

"Well," said Aidan, "maybe this is Charles, my trusted pet falcon…oh, it couldn't be. His claws would be digging into my eyes by now."

"No! Guess again!"

"Well, this couldn't be little McKenzie, could it?"

"Hmphhh…How did you know?"

"Oh, just a lucky guess," said Aidan as he turned to face her. McKenzie jumped up into his arms and hugged Aidan so tightly he could hardly breathe.

"What adventure will we go on today?"

"The first thing we need to do is get the bucket of water out of the well…it seems to be stuck." Together they looked down into the well.

"It's just stuck on that rock down there," said McKenzie matter-of-factly. "Just hold on to my legs and lower me down so I can work the bucket free."

"No!" Aidan said firmly. "We'll find another way."

"Don't be silly," said McKenzie as she crawled up on the edge of the well. "This will just take a moment." Aidan quickly but carefully pulled McKenzie away from the well.

"What are you doing?" she said as she turned to face him. "I can't reach the bucket from here!" Aidan studied her determined little face. Her blonde hair glistened

The Well

in the sunlight, and her piercing blue eyes somehow assured him that everything would be all right.

"You're pretty brave for a seven-year-old," he said. "At least wait until I have a hold of you." Aidan lifted his little friend with ease, and carefully held her in place as she reached into the well and effortlessly freed the water bucket.

"See?" said McKenzie as Aidan put her back onto the ground. "That wasn't so hard."

Aidan froze. "Do you hear that?" he asked. "It's coming from the well…"

"I'll beat you to the house!" shouted McKenzie as she darted away. There was no catching her, not with a bucket of water in his hand.

Aidan looked back at the well. The peculiar sounds had stopped, although the uneasy trembling in his legs had not. He finally turned and headed up toward the cottage, where he knew a good, hot breakfast would be waiting for him.

Aidan of Oren

CHAPTER 3

Charles the Great

The warm aroma coming from the stove swept pleasantly over Aidan as he entered. Grandmama greeted him from across the room with a wink. She was her usual cheerful self, not showing any signs of the earlier morning distraction. As Aidan joined McKenzie at the table for a hot bowl of barley, he watched as his Grandmama moved gracefully from the stove to the pantry. Always busy, always humming or singing, always giving advice. She was the smartest person in the world, Aidan was sure of it—and she was a *very* good cook.

"Hello, is there anyone home?" Lilly's voice drifted from the front door to the kitchen. She and McKenzie were Aidan's two closest friends in the world. The girls shared a room down the street at the House of Kintz, a home for orphans.

"Good morning Lilly," said Grandmama as she walked toward the door. "You're just in time for breakfast. It seems that McKenzie got the jump on you today."

"Good morning to you," said Lilly as she walked in and politely hugged Grandmama. "So then, McKenzie is here?"

"She sure is!" called Aidan from the table. "You should see how much she's eating!"

"McKenzie," said Lilly as she entered the room, "did you get all of your chores done this morning?"

McKenzie had a mouthful of food and could only mutter "uh-hummph." She took a moment to swallow, and grinned over at Lilly. "I woke up this morning while it was still dark and decided to get my chores done early."

"Alright. But next time, just let me know when you're leaving without me so I don't worry."

Aidan watched as Lilly took a seat across the table from him. He marveled at her maturity. Even though she was a year younger than he, she was always the one who could make sense out of everything. Her black silky hair, dark skin, and green eyes made her unique in all of Oren. Although a child herself, she was the mother that McKenzie never had.

Neither Lilly, nor McKenzie, nor Aidan for that matter, had ever known their parents. Many children hadn't, given the recent war. But, the three of them had been friends ever since they could remember, sharing a bond stronger than blood. When not doing their chores, they would spend every waking moment together. Often, they would venture up to the meadow, where they would lay back and look at the sky as Aidan recited the exciting stories he had heard the night before. Lilly and McKenzie loved to hear them, and would hang on every word as Aidan told the stories over and over again.

Lilly broke the silence. "Grandmama, breakfast is delicious, as always."

"Oh, thank you, Lilly. It is always nice to see the three of you together."

"We're going on an adventure today!" beamed McKenzie.

"Is that right?" asked Grandmama as she bent down and hugged her. "Just what kind of adventure do you mean?"

"I don't know," she said. "Yesterday, Aidan said we would go on an adventure. I was so excited I could hardly sleep."

"Grandmama," said Aidan, "we're going to explore the path up to the village."

"That sounds like a wonderful adventure, children. While you're exploring, would you mind terribly picking up a few things at the market?"

"But…" started Aidan.

"Of course we don't mind," interrupted Lilly as she shot a warning glance across the table. "Isn't that right, Aidan?"

"We could have an adventure at the market!" exclaimed McKenzie.

"My dear boy," started Grandmama, "is there any reason you don't want to go to the market for me?"

"It's because of the Braddock boys!" McKenzie blurted out. "They make fun of Aidan because he has reddish hair!"

Aidan, who had by this time lost his appetite, shuffled in his seat.

"Oh…" said Grandmama, "you're talking about little Eric and Kyle."

"They're not little anymore!" interrupted Aidan. "Eric is fifteen years old now!"

Lilly tried to reason with Aidan that the boys were just teasing. McKenzie was giggling and saying something about how Aidan could beat them both up, and Grandmama was speaking softly as she stood behind McKenzie, braiding her beautiful blonde hair. Aidan could not hear them, though. He had drifted off in thought to the Braddock brothers. He just knew that the moment they saw him, they would begin teasing him about his hair, calling him a sissy, but, it wouldn't stop there. They also teased him because he spent a lot of time with Lilly and McKenzie. The thought of going anywhere near them made him shudder.

Charles the Great

"Aidan!" Grandmama's stern voice brought him back to reality. "I need you to go to the market. Do you understand me?" Aidan nodded, and Grandmama's voice softened. "You're such a timid boy, Aidan. Someday you will learn that the only thing to be afraid of is well, being afraid. As for your hair, it's beautiful. Why, it's the color of fire. That's why your mother and father named you 'Aidan'. Your name means 'fire'."

"But, the Braddock brothers…"

"I know all about them and I know for a fact that the family is experiencing some difficulty. Sometimes people have to make others miserable to make them feel better about their own life. Maybe pity would be a better emotion to extend to them."

Aidan sat straight up in his seat. He was feeling much better, and started laughing. "Alright, I will be certain to let them know of my concern as they beat me into the ground!" Grandmama reached across the table and teasingly mussed his hair.

"What does my name mean?" asked McKenzie impatiently.

"And mine?" asked Lilly as politely as she could.

"McKenzie," said Grandmama as a wry smile spread across her wrinkled face, "your name means 'little warrior.'"

"Oh, my!" exclaimed Aidan. "Whoever named her sure got that one right!"

"Lilly," she continued, "your name is rooted in purity and wisdom."

"That's uncanny," said Aidan, this time more sober.

"How could two names be so accurate?"

"I counted three," said Grandmama.

McKenzie jumped out of her chair and started dancing around the room. "We're going exploring in the village!"

"Children," said Grandmama, "exploring can be great fun, but take care that you do not trespass in forbidden areas. You need to watch out for each other, and make sure you stay together. Aidan, you will see to that, won't you?"

"I will. You don't have to worry," he said with renewed confidence.

"We'll want to get started soon," said Lilly. "We may want to pack a lunch for ourselves. Grandmama, please make us a list of what you need so we don't forget anything."

"Excuse me!" came a shrill voice. Charles, Aidan's pet falcon, walked into the room. "Did anyone think to ask me about this little quest? The path up to the village can be very treacherous; we need to think this through before we just scurry off. And besides, it's a long walk, a very long walk. These little legs have to work a lot harder than yours—I don't know if I can do it." Charles paused, and ruffled his bright red feathers. "You were going to ask me to go with you …weren't you?"

Everyone laughed. Although flightless, Charles had the gift of speech. Talking animals were not uncommon in Lionsgate, but Charles was the only bird Aidan knew who could speak.

"Charles," said Aidan, "if I didn't know any better,

Charles the Great

I'd say that you're really more of a chicken than a falcon."

"I am not a chicken!" exclaimed Charles. "I am a regal falcon from the royal family of Wingdom!"

"Oh, Charles," Grandmama said, "you are such a tender bird, we may just have to eat you for lunch!" Again the room filled with laughter. Aidan was laughing so hard that he almost fell off of his chair.

"Alright, go ahead and laugh," said Charles as he turned to walk out of the room. "But if you're going to go on a journey, you'll need a scout. And, you wouldn't want to eat the scout, now, would you?"

I am a Regal Falcon from the Royal Family of Wingdom

McKenzie looked at Grandmama and whispered, "We're not really going to eat him, are we?"

Grandmama leaned down to kiss her on the forehead. "Not today, dear," she winked, "not today."

CHAPTER 4

The Hooded Man

ith Charles on his shoulder, Aidan led the way up the dusty path toward the village. As the children topped the crest of a small hill, Zorn Mountain could be seen rising in the distance.

"What a beautiful day!" exclaimed Lilly. "The mountain is very bright today. It's so clear you can even see the snow on top of it!"

"I've heard Grandmama and her friends tell stories about the mountain," said Aidan. "They say that Zorn Mountain watches over Oren so that nothing bad happens."

"Now that's ridiculous," cried Charles, who to that point had been fairly quiet. "Mountains do not protect villages. They're not human like us."

Aidan and Lilly looked at each other and tried not to laugh.

"In fact," Charles continued, "when it comes right down to it, Zorn Mountain is nothing more than just a big rock!"

McKenzie quietly walked up behind Aidan and pulled on Charles' tail feathers. "You've got a pretty long tail for a human!" she laughed.

"Stop it!" the irritated falcon screamed. "My tail is not a plaything!"

Soon, they reached the edge of the village. Many of the town women were out visiting the local shops and taking their animals to market. Children were playing in the street. However, very few men could be seen. Of the ones that were there, most of them were bandaged and badly wounded. Because of the war, most of the men had left the village to help guard the borders of Lionsgate from invaders. Aidan wanted to go and help protect their country too, but he was not old enough. The center of Oren Village was marked by a great stone building called the Hall of Judges. It was very old and all boarded up. Cracks and vines lined the outside walls; it was obvious that it had not been used for many years.

"That building scares me," said Lilly as they approached the massive gate guarding the entrance to the hall. "I wonder what used to happen here."

"Grandmama told me that the building used to be the home of the guardian," said Aidan. "The guardian was the one who made the laws and kept the peace in Oren. In fact, there used to be many guardians all around Lionsgate. But for some reason, they all suddenly left. That was many years ago."

"How very sad," said McKenzie. "I would have liked to meet him. I'll bet he was a very big man."

"Yes, me too," said Aidan, as he turned and headed to market, "but one thing is for sure, the guardian was very big and very powerful."

The Hooded Man

"Charles sure is quiet today," said Lilly, as she quickened her steps to keep up with Aidan. "Maybe he's asleep?"

"Don't make that assumption," added Aidan. "This bird talks in his sleep!"

"Well I'm not sleeping anymore, thanks to you!" shouted Charles. "Anyway, I do *not* talk in my sleep. If that were true, I'm sure I would have heard it for myself!"

Aidan stopped walking. McKenzie was not by his side. Looking back he saw that she was busy picking up rocks and putting them into her pockets. He was just about to call her back when someone else called for him.

"Hey, Aidan! I see you're hanging out with girls again!" Kyle Braddock shouted for all to hear as he jumped down from a window ledge in the Hall of Judges.

Kyle was the younger of the two irritating brothers.

"You shouldn't be in there," said Lilly. "It's not safe, you know."

Eric, the older brother, came out just behind Kyle. They walked across the courtyard and squeezed their way between the large iron bars of the main gate to where the children were standing.

"What do you know?" asked Eric. "You're just a strange looking girl. My dad says that you're the reason bad things happen around here."

Kyle walked up to Aidan and pushed him backwards. "Look, the sissy has a birdie on his shoulder!"

"I am not a birdie!" quipped Charles. "I am a falcon. As for you two filthy ragamuffins, I'd run away quickly before you stir Aidan's anger."

"Stir his anger?" said Eric and Kyle together as they towered over Aidan.

Just then, Aidan heard something whiz by his ear.

"Ouch!" said Eric as he grabbed his right shoulder. "Who threw that rock?"

"I did!" said McKenzie defiantly as she walked toward them. "And there's more where that came from if you don't leave Aidan alone."

"That's not how we should handle this!" scolded Lilly as she wrapped her arms around McKenzie, stopping her in her tracks. "Now put down the rocks."

McKenzie reluctantly obeyed. Aidan, who was desperately trying to remember how his Grandmama would want him to handle the situation, had an idea. "I'm sorry that you both have miserable lives," he stammered. The brothers, together in disbelief, turned their attention to Aidan, who continued to speak awkwardly, "I'm sorry for you and I pity you."

"That's not quite how I would have handled it," whispered Charles in Aidan's ear. "Now we're going to get beat up for sure!"

The brothers, with their fists clenched, moved even closer to Aidan. Suddenly, they stopped. Their eyes opened wide with fright. They turned, and ran away as fast as they could.

"That went well," said Charles. "They must have perceived that I wasn't playing around with them!"

Aidan could hear a growing commotion behind him. He turned around to take a look, knowing immediately that something was dreadfully wrong. "Don't move!" he yelled as he gathered Lilly and McKenzie close to him.

"I can see people scattering behind us! They seem to be running for their lives. Something's coming."

"What is it?" cried Charles, who immediately tucked his head under Aidan's collar and demanded "Hide me!"

Aidan stood his ground, with Lilly and McKenzie standing behind him, each holding one of his arms. As the wave of scattering people approached, Aidan froze. Walking slowly toward them was a very tall man wearing a hooded cloak. "Don't look at him!" Aidan whispered to the girls. "Stay behind me, and keep your eyes closed until I tell you it's safe!"

The hooded man walked up to where Aidan stood and looked down at him. The townspeople had all left the area. Aidan was very afraid, but did not run.

The tall stranger raised his hand and pointed all around. A deep, growling voice rolled out from under the hood. "Why don't you run away like the rest of them?" He spoke slowly and deliberately.

Aidan stared up into the hood without saying a word. What he saw frightened him horribly. Why wouldn't his feet move? He wanted so badly to run like the others.

"What is your name?" asked the hooded man.

Aidan swallowed hard, and then mustered, "I am Aidan, Aidan of Oren."

"I seek the child of Oren," mused the stranger. "Could it be that I have found him?"

"No!" shouted McKenzie, still covering her eyes and standing behind Aidan. "There are hundreds of children in the village of Oren! Go and pester someone else!"

The hooded man let out an evil laugh. "Who is hiding behind you?"

Aidan instinctively took a step backwards and extended his arms to shield the girls.

The Hooded Man

The hooded man reached his long arm toward the children. "The little one seems to be feisty. Bring her to me."

Aidan glared up into the hood. A wave of heat rushed over his body, and he felt as if his blood was about to boil. Then the earth began to quake, slowly at first, but quickly building in intensity.

The hooded man looked up to the darkening sky, and then back down at Aidan. As the hooded man withdrew his arm, the quaking stopped.

"Perhaps you *are* the child of Oren," he said as he turned to walk away. Looking back, he added, "Another day, Aidan of Oren. Another day."

After the hooded man left, Aidan turned to his friends and asked, "Are the two of you alright?"

"We're fine," said Lilly. "I don't understand what just happened."

Aidan of Oren

"I do!" insisted McKenzie. "Aidan wanted to protect us. And the land wanted to protect him."

"That's silly!" scolded Charles as he pulled his head from under Aidan's collar. "The land doesn't protect people! It was simply a well-timed tremor."

"I don't know about all that," said Aidan, wiping beads of sweat from his brow. "What I do know is that we need to hurry and get the things for Grandmama before it gets too late."

Meanwhile, behind a nearby building, the Braddock brothers stood side by side, trembling. They had witnessed in disbelief everything that had transpired. Quietly, they left the area to go find their father.

CHAPTER 5

True Courage

The remainder of the day went by without incident. Lilly, McKenzie, and Charles made great light of the hooded man and the way he talked. Aidan, however, could not laugh with them. They hadn't seen what was under the hood, but Aidan had. He would never forget the twisted face, and the bloodshot, bulging eyes that seemed to look right through him. He pondered on the fantastic events of the day, and wondered how it was possible for him to stand and face the hooded man when everyone else ran away. That just wasn't like him.

As the sun began to set, Grandmama came in from the garden, where she had been working the better part of the day. She was washing her hands when Aidan walked up behind her and gave her a big hug.

"Oh, how nice!" she said as she put away the hand towel. "I don't often get greeted like this. What's wrong, dear?"

"How do you know something is wrong?"

"Well, you hugged me in a manner that says you're very glad to be home and your face has that worried look." Grandmama walked across the room and started a pot of hot tea. She looked over at him and asked, "Has something frightened you?"

"I just have never seen anything like the man that we met in the market today." He paused for a moment. "Yes…yes, I was frightened. In fact, I have never been so frightened in all my life!"

"Fiddlesticks!" said Charles as he walked into the room. "It wasn't all that bad! Why, it was just a tall man with an oversized blanket on his head."

"How would you know?" quipped Aidan. "Your head was under my collar the whole time and you shook like a leaf!"

Grandmama laughed and said, "I've got some breading in the pantry. Perhaps we will have fried chicken tonight after all!"

"Well, excuse me!" exclaimed Charles as he pranced across the floor on his way out the door. "I was just trying to help. Would you please stop talking about eating me!"

Grandmama poured a cup of hot tea and sat down beside Aidan as he stared out across the table, not really looking at anything. "I saw his face," he said quietly.

"It's alright now," Grandmama said as she put her arm around him. "The hooded man is gone."

Aidan turned and looked at his grandmama. "How did you know I saw a hooded man?"

"Oh, news travels fast," she laughed. "I heard that the Braddock brothers saw the whole thing; nearly scared them to death!"

"That's what I don't understand. If everyone else ran

away, why didn't I run, too?"

"My child, fear is nothing more than concern for oneself. True courage, on the other hand, comes from concern for others. The bravest men in the world are those with tender hearts. Today, you stood before the stranger because you were protecting your friends." Grandmama leaned over and placed a kiss on Aidan's forehead. "Remember, the building blocks of courage are these: love, compassion, and a tender heart."

Aidan took a deep breath. "You know, I sort of made a fool out of myself today in front of Eric and Kyle."

"I heard about what you said to them. What I was trying to teach you was that you must understand what someone else may be going through before you judge him too harshly. Compassion is the key. You'll do better next time, I'm sure."

"So, do you know who the tall man is?"

"I'm not sure, there is a legend…"

"He said he was looking for the child of Oren."

Grandmama's smile dimmed a little. "Are you sure of his words, Aidan?"

"Yes. He looked straight at me and said it. He even said he believes that I am the child of Oren. Then, the most amazing thing happened."

"I know, dear," said Grandmama with worry in her voice. "We felt the earth shaking all the way over here. Tell me, Aidan, did he threaten you or the girls?"

"Why, in fact, he did! He noticed McKenzie behind me and reached for her. My face felt very hot, but I didn't do anything, really!"

Aidan of Oren

"Didn't you, though?" Grandmama said, as she sipped her tea and looked off into the distance.

CHAPTER 6

Quilting by the Fire

ater that evening, Aidan was washing dishes for Grandmama when he saw one of her friends, Nesta, coming up the path toward the cottage. 'This must be story night,' he thought to himself. 'Won't Lilly and McKenzie be excited to hear something new tomorrow!' He quickly cleaned up and went to his bedroom to prepare for the night. Charles was perched in the corner with his head tucked back into his wings, but Aidan noticed that his eyes were open. Aidan put on a clean nightshirt and noticed that the falcon's eyes were following him as he moved around the room.

"Hello Charles," said Aidan. "Why are you—"

"Oh! *Now* you want to say hello!" Charles interrupted. "What's it going to be, Aidan? Are you going to talk to me or are you going to eat me?"

"We were just kidding," laughed Aidan. "You shouldn't be so sensitive!" Charles just ruffled his feathers.

Just then Grandmama walked into Aidan's room with Nesta at her side. Nesta was a funny, round little lady who usually was as bubbly and happy as could be. However, tonight she seemed preoccupied. As Grandmama was saying goodnight to Aidan, Nesta said nothing. This was very odd.

Aidan could hear the chairs being brought together in the fireplace room. He crept out of bed so he could watch the activities through a crack in his door. The women lit a great fire and various candles around the room. Just then, another of Grandmama's friends arrived. It was Glenna, a very thin and frail woman who loved to talk about her dreams. Just behind her came Winnie, a large and imposing woman, who was often difficult to deal with due to her unyielding personality.

Quilting by the Fire

Each of the women brought out her favorite quilt and sat silently in a circle around the fireplace. Aidan watched with great anticipation. This is how it always started. They would quilt for a while, and then the floodgates would open and they would talk into the wee hours of the morning.

"I had another dream last night," said Glenna, breaking the silence.

"I had a dream also!" shouted Nesta. "Oh, let me tell mine first! Glenna always gets to tell her dreams, and I rarely have them at all!"

"Alright," said Grandmama softly, "if Glenna doesn't mind, go ahead and tell your dream."

Glenna nodded. "No, there isn't any hurry. We've got all night."

Nesta squirmed with excitement as she began to talk. "Last night, I had a dream about a giant sugar muffin. It was huge, about the size of Winnie…"

"Is that really necessary?" asked Winnie, a bit perturbed.

"Oh, I'm sorry. I was just trying to give you an idea of the breadth of the giant muffin," explained Nesta. Winnie shot her a warning look, but Nesta continued on. "Anyway, in my dream, I had ventured back to the stream to wash some clothes when I heard something behind me. I turned around, and to my surprise the sugar muffin was following me! I went to the market, and again the sugar muffin followed me. Every time I turned around, the sugar muffin was there. I woke up

in a cold sweat! Seren, you're a teller of dreams, what does all of this mean?"

Aidan had heard the women of the village refer to his Grandmama by her proper name before, but he had forgotten how beautiful the name was.

"Seren, what does it mean?" Nesta persisted. "I'm worried!"

Grandmama stopped quilting and looked soberly at Nesta. An awkward silence filled the room as she sat back in her rocking chair and said, "Nesta, this is a very significant dream. I will reveal to you its meaning…but, only if you must know."

"Tell me!" insisted Nesta, "I've been worrying about this all day now!"

"Well," Grandmama started. "It means...no, I can't. It might scare you."

"You have to tell me!" cried Nesta, almost frantic. "I just knew that the dream had a meaning! Is something horrible going to happen?"

"No," Grandmama said softly. "The dream means simply this. You worry about food too much!"

All of the ladies around the circle burst into laughter, even Nesta. "Seren, you tricked me!" she said.

Winnie was laughing the loudest. It was a good thing, because Aidan was laughing, too. His hand was over his mouth to muffle the sound, and he moved away from the crack in the door in case someone looked in his direction.

"Glenna," said Grandmama. "Why don't you tell us about your dream?"

"Alright," she started. "I had the most wonderful dream about elves..."

"Oh, I love elves!" said Nesta.

"Nesta!" said Winnie. "Let Glenna tell her dream, please!" Her voice softened, and her face took on the demeanor of a little girl. "They're always so enchanting—I love to hear about them."

Glenna started again. "The little elves were preparing for a celebration. They sang and they danced, and they recited a special poem, which they kept saying over and over. They called it the wish poem."

"What's so special about that?" asked Nesta. "We all know that elves always speak in rhymes."

"This was different," said Glenna. "The elf poem

seemed to have great significance. Let me tell you what they said."

As Glenna started reciting the wish poem, Aidan closed his eyes and listened. What beautiful words. Wouldn't Lilly and McKenzie be thrilled to hear this! When he opened his eyes, Aidan looked over at Grandmama and noticed that she was looking in his direction. He quickly pulled his head back. Maybe she hadn't seen him. Aidan quietly slipped into bed and pulled the covers up over his head. "A wish poem!" he thought, "how fantastic!" He silently recited the words over and over again, putting them to memory, as he slowly drifted off to sleep.

CHAPTER 7

The Legend of Gorgon

The sound of creaking hinges awakened Aidan with a start. The front door was slowly opening. He could hear footsteps and voices. Aidan jumped out of bed and peeked through his door. He saw the glowing embers in the fireplace. It was very late.

"Come in, Helfin," said Grandmama. "We were expecting you." Aidan peeked as far to his left as he could, and was surprised to see Helfin Kintz standing in the doorway. She and her husband, Carl, owned the House of Kintz, the town orphanage. Carl also served as the local blacksmith. As far back as Aidan could remember Helfin had never before attended one of the quilting sessions. Helfin was a stark woman with large, bony cheeks and haunting, recessed eyes. Her demeanor was pleasant, yet reserved. Grandmama pulled up a chair so that Helfin could join the others in the circle. She seemed out of place and uncomfortable.

"Relax. You're with friends now," said Glenna, who was sitting beside her.

"It's times like this that I wish I had taken up quilting," she said awkwardly. "But, we're not here to talk

51

about cloth and thread, are we?"

"I wish we were," said Grandmama.

"It's because of the hooded man, isn't it?" asked Glenna.

Aidan's eyes widened, but he didn't dare move. He could hear every word.

"I've invited Helfin to join us tonight. The time has come," said Grandmama.

"No," said Winnie. "The children are too young! Surely now is not the time for—"

"Winnie," interrupted Glenna, "destiny chooses its own time."

"Well, I don't know about the rest of you," said Winnie, "but I don't have a whole lot of patience with a man who walks through town scaring everybody."

"You speak bravely from the comfort of your chair," said Grandmama. "Maybe you should seek him out and tell him how you feel in person." Winnie simply shrugged her shoulders, trying hard to show that she wasn't afraid. But everyone could see that she was.

"It's alright to be afraid," said Glenna softly.

"Does he even have a name?" asked Nesta.

"There is a legend," started Helfin, and then she paused.

"Go on, tell them. It's time for them to know the full story," said Grandmama.

Helfin regained her composure and started again. "There's a legend of a man from Goth who roams the land. His name is Gorgon. He was once a beautiful child and son of a king. One day in his travels, he met an imp sitting on the bank of a river. The strange little creature was looking at its reflection in the water, and seemed sad. Gorgon knew that imps were best left alone, but his curiosity got the best of him. He approached the little creature slowly, fascinated by its gruesome appearance. Suddenly, the creature turned its head toward Gorgon. The young prince became immediately entranced by the pale blue eyes of the little creature. It asked him this question:

'What do you see when you look at me?'

"Gorgon laughed at the imp, and in doing so made a horrible mistake. All of his riches could not buy the one thing he needed most at that moment: compassion. Thus, in a poorly timed attempt at humor, he said these fateful words:

'I see a face that would strike fear into any man. You obviously have no friends.'

The little creature looked back into the river and said,

'So shall it be. So shall it be.'

"When Gorgon knelt down by the river to get a drink of water, his heart turned cold as he saw his reflection. The young prince's face was now the face he had scorned. It was too horrible even for him to gaze upon. He hurried back to his homeland, only to be shunned by his friends, and even by his own family. He became an outcast, a nomad. His heart turned dark, and his bitterness turned him to a life of pure hatred."

Aidan, still peeking through the door, could not believe what he was hearing.

"How very sad," said Nesta.

"Don't be sad!" warned Helfin. "Be afraid! Whenever the hooded man appears, destruction soon follows. There is no good in him. I fear for the child of Oren."

"Why is he here, then?"

"He did not come on his own accord. He was sent on a mission."

"Who sent him?" Nesta began fidgeting.

"The Lord of Dunjon," she replied coldy.

"No!" shouted Winnie. "It's too soon!"

"Seren," said Helfin abruptly, "how old is the boy now?"

"He turns thirteen in two days," said Grandmama as she began to wring her hands nervously.

"The time has come," Helfin said. "If the Lord of

Dunjon can stop the prophecy from being fulfilled, peace will never be restored and all will be lost."

Aidan's eyes widened with fear and excitement. Were they really talking about him? Who was the Lord of Dunjon?

"Do any of you remember the prophecy?" asked Helfin as she looked around the room. "The boy must find the elves, and soon. Let me refresh your memories.

> 'When the hooded man first appears,
> A child will arise of thirteen years.
> A child of fire, of Oren pride
> Wisdom, and a warrior, at his side.
> To travel up the way of sorrow,
> As longest day is nigh the morrow.
> From elves to learn the ancient ways,
> And secrets told from yonder days.
> Destined to set the guardians free,
> To harvest peace from sea to sea.'"

"This doesn't make any sense!" cried Nesta. "How can he possibly find the elves?" She popped up out of her chair and began pacing around the room. "No one even knows if they really exist!"

"Oh, they exist," replied Glenna.

Nesta was beginning to lose control. "No one has ever seen an elf!"

"I have," said Glenna, "in my dreams."

Aidan could hardly contain himself behind the door. Was he supposed to look for the mysterious elves? His imagination began to get the better of him.

"The mountain will be his beacon," said Glenna, "and

the map will be his compass. Nesta, we've all known for a long time that this day would come. Don't worry." All of the women soberly nodded.

Nesta sat back down in her chair and tried to calm down. "I just don't know about these so-called prophecies. We're trusting something that even we do not fully understand."

"We have no choice," said Helfin. "Sometimes life demands a leap of faith. Seren, is the child ready?"

Grandmama cupped her hands on her lap and looked into them for what seemed like a long time. Then she spoke words that Aidan would never forget. "My friends, Aidan has the courage of a lion, the spirit of the wind, and the wisdom of a king. He is ready for the journey."

Aidan put his hand over his mouth so no one would hear his gasp. Surely they weren't talking about him!

'The courage of a lion?' he thought to himself half amused. He couldn't even stand up to the Braddock brothers! This didn't make any sense.

"I don't want to alarm anyone," said Glenna as she got up from her chair to pour herself a fresh cup of tea, "but the summer solstice is only four days away."

"What's the summer solitude?" asked Nesta awkwardly.

"It's the summer *solstice*, Nesta. It's the day of the year that the sun shines the longest. All of the days before and after the summer solstice are shorter."

"Oh," said Nesta.

"Four days," sighed Grandmama. "So little time…"

Four days until what? He pressed his face harder to the door, trying desperately to hear everything that was being said. What journey? However, the voices were starting to sound distant. The light in the fireplace room started to dim. Everything was going dark.

CHAPTER 8

McKenzie's Gift

idan, let's go!" shouted a little voice in his ear.

"What?!" Aidan sat straight up in bed. It was morning. The sun had just risen and was shining directly in his eyes. He could hear McKenzie and Lilly giggling in the background.

"How did I get here?" he asked incredulously. "I was over there, by the door…"

"What's all the racket?" asked an irritated Charles from his perch. "Can't you see we're trying to get some sleep?"

"Good morning, Aidan," said Grandmama as she entered the room. "If I remember right, you were going to play out by the meadow today."

"Oh…" he said, still trying to get the cobwebs out of his head. "Yes, but Grandmama, I wanted to speak to you about…"

"We'll talk later. Your friends are here and anxious to go out and play," said Grandmama. "I can't think of a better day for the three of you to be together." Grandmama gave him an approving kiss on the forehead and left his room. Aidan jumped out of bed and prepared for breakfast.

Outside, the warm summer air smelled fresh. Lilly and McKenzie were in the best of moods, but not Aidan. He was haunted by what he had heard last night. Had he dreamed it all? Was any of it real? He had so many questions. Somehow he knew that from this day forward, his life would never be the same.

"Let's hurry to the meadow," said McKenzie, as she took his hand. "I'd love to hear a new story."

"I think that the excitement from yesterday's adventure should last us for a while, McKenzie," Lilly said. "Let's not ask too much of Aidan. He did almost get beat up."

McKenzie picked up a stick and waved it in the air. "Next time I see that mean man, I'll poke his eye out!"

"Easy does it!" said Aidan as he pulled the stick out of McKenzie's hand. "You'll poke *my* eye out with that thing if you're not careful!"

They walked until they reached the top of a rising hill, where they had a scenic view of the country. This spot was their sanctuary.

"Do you want to play hide and seek?" asked McKenzie as she tugged at Aidan's arm.

"McKenzie," said Lilly, "can't you see that something is on his mind? Anyway, you know that it's no fun to play hide and seek with Aidan. He's too good. I've never known anyone who could hide like he can. It's not fair, really."

"Are you saying that I'm a cheater?" Aidan laughed.

"Let's wrestle!" squealed McKenzie as she ran over and grabbed Aidan's legs, knocking both him and Lilly to the ground. The three of them wrestled, laughing hysterically. Lilly somehow managed to free herself from the wrestling match. "Aidan, I have something for you," she said, sitting down with her basket on her lap.

"What's in the basket?" asked McKenzie.

"You'll see…" Lilly reached inside and pulled out a beautiful leather necklace. "I've been working on this for the last few weeks. I thought Aidan might like it."

"Oh, thank you," said Aidan as he gave her a big hug. "What is this for?"

"Tomorrow is your birthday. I made this for you to wear around your neck."

"I've got something for you, too!" chimed McKenzie as she reached into her pocket.

"Another gift? Did the two of you plan this?"

"No," said McKenzie as she dug deeper into her pocket. "Wait, it's in here somewhere." Dirt, small stones, and half of a beetle began to fall out of her pocket. "I got it!" McKenzie proudly pulled her hand out of her pocket and presented her gift to Aidan.

"What is it?" asked Lilly. "I can't see anything except for a pile of dirt!"

Aidan sifted through the dirt in McKenzie's hand. "I feel something," he said, startled. Aidan slowly removed something solid from her hand. "I hope it's not the other half of that beetle."

"That's disgusting!" said Lilly with a giggle. McKenzie just watched, and waited.

"A rock!" Aidan exclaimed.

"It's no ordinary rock," McKenzie said as she puffed out her little chest. "It's the prettiest rock in the world!" Aidan wiped the dusty rock on his pants, and then polished it up with his shirt. To get a good look at it, Aidan held it up to the sunlight.

"Oohhhhh!" cried Lilly. "Whatever in the world is that?" Aidan was speechless. The rock *was* beautiful. It was flat and translucent red, just like a ruby. But, even more amazing was how the sunlight, when it hit the rock, split into seven small beams.

"Look at how it divides the light!" said Aidan.

"I didn't know it could do that," McKenzie said. "I just thought it was pretty."

"Where did you get it?" asked Lilly. "That is the most beautiful rock I have ever seen."

"I told you it was the prettiest rock in the world!" said McKenzie with a big grin. "I found it in the rubble by the Hall of Judges in the village. It was just too pretty to leave laying on the ground, so I put it in my pocket."

"Why didn't you say anything?" inquired Aidan.

"Because I forgot about it," said McKenzie. "But now, I can give you a gift, too, just like Lilly did."

"Thank you both," said Aidan as he leaned over and hugged his friends. "Now I have something for you!"

"Something for us?" asked Lilly suspiciously.

"Yes," said Aidan with a big grin. "I have a new story for you."

CHAPTER 9

The Wish Poem

Astory!" squealed McKenzie, her eyes wide open in anticipation. Aidan paused for a moment, trying to build the suspense.

"Go on, tell us," said Lilly. "We haven't got all day, you know."

"Alright, alright," laughed Aidan. "Last night I heard the strangest and most wonderful story about elves. When elves talk, it's always in rhyme."

"I already know that," said McKenzie. "What else did you learn?"

Aidan gave McKenzie a curious glance. "Anyway, as I was saying, elves always talk in sentences that rhyme. I memorized one of their rhymes last night!"

"But..." McKenzie pleaded.

"McKenzie! Aidan is trying to tell us a story. Interrupting like that is rude. Now, please be quiet."

McKenzie just stared up into the sky with her lips held tightly together and her hand over her mouth.

"So the elves talk in rhymes? Oh, how exciting," continued Lilly. "How does the rhyme go?"

Aidan of Oren

"Alright," said Aidan. "I'll tell you the rhyme. It might not make a lot of sense to you and me…I think it's just the way they communicate."

"That's fine, just tell us!"

"Ok, it goes something like this:

> Make a little wish,
> Hold it in your hand;
> Kneel to the ground,
> And rub it in the sand.
> Look up to the heavens,
> And there pronounce your name.
> The wind will grant your wish,
> But you'll never be the same."

Just as Aidan finished reciting the poem, clouds appeared from over the mountain, blocking the warmth and light of the sun's rays. A strange wind started blowing in from the east.

"Oh," said Lilly as she sat straight up. "That gave me goose bumps."

Aidan looked up toward Zorn Mountain. Was that to be his beacon? The words he heard the night before came flooding back to him.

"Hey!" said Lilly. "Are you listening to me?"

Torn away from his thoughts, Aidan was startled to see Lilly standing right in front of him. "I've been talking to you! You seem to have drifted off. Is everything alright?"

Gathering his bearings, Aidan took the hands of Lilly and McKenzie and sat them down in the meadow. "I need to talk to you both," he said.

"Another story!" shouted McKenzie.

"No, this one's not a story…well maybe it is. Can the two of you keep a secret?" The two girls nodded in anticipation. "McKenzie," he started, "do you remember yesterday morning when we were out by the well?"

"Yes," she said slowly.

"After we drew the water from the well and headed for the cottage, we heard something, didn't we?"

"Yes," she said again, now starting to smile a bit.

"Can you tell me what it was that we heard?"

"Are you sure you want to listen to me now?"

Aidan was holding his breath. Lilly looked confused. "It was the elves."

"Stop telling stories!" Lilly scolded. "Aidan is trying to ask you a serious question."

"Easy, Lilly," said Aidan. "Let her speak."

"As I was saying," McKenzie got up and walked behind Aidan, "it was the elves we heard that morning. You can hear them from the well, if you listen. They talk in the most marvelous little voices, always rhyming, just like you said. I could have recited the wish poem for you, I've heard it many times…but you didn't want to hear from me."

"She's right," said Aidan as he glanced over to Lilly. "The elves do exist. Last night, Grandmama and her friends talked about them. They're real!"

"Have the two of you gone mad?"

"I know it's hard to believe, but it's true. There's more, something's happening. I think it's what Grandmama calls destiny."

"How far away is destiny?" asked McKenzie.

Lilly looked deeply into Aidan's eyes. "Does this have anything to do with your parents?"

"Do your parents live in destiny?" asked McKenzie.

Aidan drew his friends close and hugged them. "Yes, McKenzie, I believe my parents live in destiny, but I don't know if this has anything to do with them. All I know is that I'm supposed to go on some kind of journey."

"You're not going to leave us!" shouted McKenzie.

"Aidan, are you really talking about leaving?" asked Lilly in a calm yet deeply concerned voice.

"I don't know. From what I heard last night, it sounds like I'm going to have to find something…"

"I'm good at finding things!" pleaded McKenzie.

The Wish Poem

"You must take us with you!"

Aidan reached over and hugged her. "I would never leave without the two of you. You are more than family could ever be to me. But, think about this. If the elves are real, then maybe other things we've heard about in the stories are real as well. Castles and dragons are all fun to talk about, but what about the others? What about the trolls? They'll dance around you until you are hypnotized into a trance, and then they'll suck the very life out of you through your eyes. What about the seething loxi? Their hair is so long, you can't tell if you're looking at the back or the front of one of them, until they bare their horrific teeth, and then it's too late. And, what about the Dead Forest? Remember the stories about the grotesque creatures that inhabit it?"

Lilly and McKenzie tried to look as if they weren't concerned, but Aidan could sense their anxiety.

"How could I possibly put the two of you in danger? Maybe I should just forget the whole thing."

"You will most certainly go, if that is what is in your heart!" scolded Lilly. "Destiny does not call on everyone. When it does call, you answer. Do you understand me? It's settled, you go where you must, and we will follow."

Aidan thought silently for a moment. "But," he said, "I don't know."

"Aidan, you need us," said Lilly.

"Yes! You need us," chimed in McKenzie. "We're not afraid of anything, as long as we're together. Let us go with you, Aidan," she begged.

"You're not making this easy for me."

"The decision whether or not we go with you is ours, not yours," Lilly said.

"Alright…I will talk to Grandmama tonight. I think she'll understand. Somehow, she always does. Surely she will need to discuss this with Carl and Helfin. One thing is certain, though. The journey that beckons is one we will take together."

Lilly held McKenzie close to her, and said excitedly, "Yes, we'll go together."

McKenzie looked up at Aidan. "Will we travel toward destiny?"

"Yes, my little princess," he said. "We will most certainly travel toward destiny."

CHAPTER 10

The Dragon Chest

he children spent the rest of the afternoon talking excitedly about what lay ahead of them. Their joy was based in the mere fact that, if nothing else, at least the three of them would be together.

The sun was just setting as Aidan arrived back at Grandmama's cottage. Walking in the door, he could smell beef stew— his favorite.

"Why, hello Aidan!" greeted Grandmama. "Tonight, I've made something special for you."

Aidan walked up to Grandmama and gave her a big hug. "You are the best Grandmama in the whole world. I have never wanted for anything."

"Aidan, that's not a hard thing to do for a boy who doesn't need much. You are easily pleased, which makes my job simple, not to mention pleasant."

"Excuse me!" said Charles as he walked into the room. "I do hate to interrupt this touching moment, but I'd really like to know why I was left behind today."

Aidan laughed as he sat down at the kitchen table. "Charles, when I left this morning, you were still sleeping. I didn't wake you for fear that I might scare you to death, and you wouldn't want that, now would you?"

Charles opened his mouth, but Grandmama cut in.

"Charles was a big help to me today, Aidan. Thank you for leaving him here for me to talk to as I did my cleaning. He has so many interesting stories to tell, we had a splendid time."

"Well, I am a very good orator," Charles said as he puffed out his chest. "It's too bad that you missed out, Aidan."

Aidan threw a biscuit over to Charles. "Yes," he said jokingly, "too bad for me."

After dinner, Aidan joined Grandmama in the fireplace room, sitting at her feet with Charles nestled into his shoulder. He had many questions for Grandmama.

The Dragon Chest

Aidan pulled the leather necklace Lilly had given him out of his pocket and put it around his neck. "What do you think of my gift from Lilly?" he asked. "She made it just for me. Isn't it beautiful?"

Grandmama leaned forward. "What a lovely necklace," she said tenderly. "Lilly certainly has a gift for creating beauty." As she was admiring the necklace, Aidan reached into his pocket and pulled out his other surprise.

"That's not all. Look at what McKenzie gave me," he said proudly as he handed the prize to Grandmama. "Isn't it the most beautiful rock you've ever seen?"

Grandmama was silent as Aidan laid it in her trembling hands. She closely examined the strange rock, and then held it to her chest. She closed her eyes for a moment.

"Where did you get this?" she asked softly.

"Actually, McKenzie found it near the Hall of Judges over by the market."

"Does it divide the light?"

"Well," Aidan said a bit nervously, "actually, it does. But, how did you know?"

"Because..." Grandmama drew a deep breath. "Because it is not a rock at all."

"What is it then?" said Aidan. "Is it a giant ruby? Is it valuable?"

Grandmama laughed. "I guess you're old enough to know the truth. Although this is not a ruby, it certainly is valuable." She leaned over toward the young lad and whispered in his ear, "In fact, it's priceless!"

Isn't it the most Beautiful Rock you've ever seen?

Aidan held his breath, waiting for her to continue. "What you have found is the scale of a dragon."

Aidan felt a little disoriented. "What are you talking about, Grandmama? There are no such things as dragons! Those are just stories, they're not real, are they?"

"Of course they're real," said Grandmama. "Just what

stories are you talking about? Have you been listening to the conversations that I've had with my friends? If I'm correct, I believe they only come over late at night, way past your bedtime."

"It sure is chilly for a summer's night, isn't it?" he said in a weak effort to change the subject. He was excited and confused at the same time. He moved over to the fireplace, and sat down on the hearth.

"Yes it is," agreed Grandmama. "Could you get a blanket for me? It's getting colder outside. There is a quilt in the chest at the foot of my bed. Would you mind?"

What had she said? The chest! Aidan's heart raced. The chest in Grandmama's room was the only thing he was forbidden to touch. He had often gone into her room when she was away to market and sat in front of the chest, marveling at its craftsmanship. The front panels on each side of the lock displayed ornate carvings of dragons, each facing one another, with fire spewing from their mouths. The left carving was stained black, as if it were branded into the wood. The right carving was composed of white ash, oddly beautiful in its simplicity. The lid of the chest was even more fascinating. Made purely of tree branches, each bent over at the precise angle necessary to fit with the next, it created a semi-circular labyrinth of craftsman perfection. The oval-shaped gaps between the branches each displayed the carving of an eye. Regardless where you stood in the room, when you looked at the chest, the chest appeared to be looking back at you.

And now, Grandmama had given Aidan permission to open the chest. Was she too tired to know what she was saying? Aidan struggled with this thought as he walked slowly into her room. Every footstep he took seemed louder than the last, and he just knew that she would call him back before he had the chance to open it. Reaching the foot of the bed, Aidan knelt down in front of the magnificent chest.

The room was dark, lit only by the light of the fire in the next room. The eyes between the branches reflected what little light there was, and seemed to glow in the dark. With trembling hands he lifted the lid. It was heavier than he had anticipated, but it opened smoothly. On the top, just as Grandmama had said, was the quilt.

Aidan pulled the neatly-folded quilt out of the chest.

The Dragon Chest

This was the one she had worked on during her storytelling evenings with her friends. It was a beautiful quilt. Aidan looked back at the open chest. Should he venture further inside? He had never given Grandmama a reason not to trust him and he would not start now. He gently closed the lid and took the quilt into the fireplace room.

"Thank you, Aidan," she said as he unfolded the quilt and laid it over her. Then he heard something drop to the floor. He looked down and noticed a rolled up paper tied with a red ribbon. Grandmama noticed it, too. "Oh, I've been looking for that," she said with a hint of mischief in her voice. "Why don't you open that up so we can take a peek at it?"

CHAPTER 11

The Map

The moon shone brightly through the nearby window, lighting up the fireplace room. Aidan picked up the scroll, and with trembling hands removed the ribbon and spread it open. The paper unrolled awkwardly in his hands. It was old and stiff, as if it had not been opened in many years. Aidan gasped as the contents of the paper came into focus by the moonlight.

"It's a map!" he exclaimed. "Wherever did you get this?"

"Oh, I've had it for a while. What do you see?"

Aidan's eyes darted back and forth across the parchment. "Look! There's Oren!" he said excitedly, pointing to the lower left side of the page. Just below Oren was the Botham Sea. "That would be south!" he said, tracing a path from Oren down to the sea with his finger. Grandmama just nodded in agreement, sipping her tea. Again, he placed his finger on the map, starting in Oren, following the path he knew as Sorrow's Way. Aidan ran his finger along this route, north to Zorn Mountain, then northwest through the Dead Forest and the Woods of Didacus toward the Valley of the Elves.

The Map

"Now we know where the elves live! The Valley of the Elves!" Aidan exclaimed.

"So you were listening…"

Aidan looked up, but could not utter a word.

"It's alright," said Grandmama as she smiled warmly. "I saw you looking through the crack in the door. It's time that you understand your destiny."

"My destiny?"

"Yes, precious one. You have always known that you are special, you just didn't know why."

"What is this all about? It seems so confusing."

"There is a prophecy that foretells of your destiny. Your destiny, the prophecy, and the war are all entwined." Her eyes slowly drifted off to a faraway place. "Long ago, even before I was born, the world was at peace. Great guardians lived among us. They worked with the people to write laws, and they were powerful enough to enforce them. One day, the guardians just left. No one knows where they went, and no one knows why. Over the years, war broke out as country after country fell to greedy and ambitious men. Families were broken apart and thrown into slavery. Lionsgate is the only country left that is still free. That's why so many of our men gather at the southern border of Braggadon, and at the northern border of Olsburg. The men fight to protect us, but they are slowly losing the battle. That is why the guardians must be found."

"What do you mean?" asked Aidan. "Why are we losing?"

"We are quite simply outnumbered."

Aidan was becoming frustrated. "Then what about the guardians? Why don't they come back?"

"That is the great mystery, my dear boy. Nobody knows. But there is an ancient prophecy that tells of them."

"Yes! The one that tells how the elves will help a child of Oren find the guardians!"

Grandmama's eyes twinkled and a wry smile broke across her face. "You listen well. Yes, the guardians must be found, or Lionsgate will fall, and all will be lost! But first, you must find the elves and learn the ancient ways. They are partners with nature and possess skills we cannot teach you. You are special, Aidan, in ways that you do not yet understand. Only you can find the guardians and bring them back."

Aidan shook his head. "I'm supposed to find the elves, learn from them, and then find the guardians and bring them back here?"

"Yes," said Grandmama, sipping her tea.

"I'm confused. Wouldn't it save time if I were simply to find the guardians instead?"

Startled, Grandmama spilled some of her tea down the front of her. "Aidan! One cannot simply approach the guardians! They are very powerful, massive, majestic beings. As amazing as that scale is that McKenzie found, imagine the beast that lies beneath thousands of them!"

"Wait! You told me that the rock I have was the scale of a dragon."

"My dear boy, the guardians *are* dragons! There isn't a person alive who could approach them without being destroyed! That's why you must find the elves! Only they can prepare you to find and stand in the presence of the guardians."

"But, I thought the guardians used to live among the people as law givers."

"Yes, but that was hundreds of years ago. For some reason, they have reverted back to their primal state.

No one knows why."

Aidan's head was spinning. How could he be the chosen one of the prophecy? "I don't think I can do this, Grandmama. I'm not strong enough or big enough."

"Don't worry Aidan," she said. "I know you have had a tough time with the Braddock boys, but now you will learn how special you are. You must believe in yourself and take your place. Know that you will have the courage to do the right thing when the time comes."

"I will try to be strong for you, Grandmama," Aidan said. "Tell me more. What about the hooded man? Does Gorgon have anything to do with all of this?"

Grandmama sighed heavily; she was getting sleepy. "Gorgon was sent to stop you."

"But there's a prophecy. Are you saying that I may not succeed?"

"Nothing happens by chance, my dear. The future is what you make of it."

Aidan had a very uneasy feeling in the pit of his stomach. "So, I could fail?"

"Yes," said Grandmama, "but you might also succeed. You have natural talents. The prophecy proves you have the potential and provides you with guidance, but ultimately success or failure depends on you."

The night was getting long, and her eyes were getting heavy. "Keep your focus, boy. Find the elves...find the...elves..." Grandmama could not keep her eyes open any longer.

Aidan tucked in the blanket around her neck and shoulders and kissed her on the forehead.

Aidan of Oren

He went into his bedroom and lay down, wondering what the new day would bring. He was now certain that a wonderous and mysterious journey awaited him. His mind drifted to Lilly and McKenzie. He had not told Grandmama of his desire to take them with him. He rolled over, trying to find a comfortable position to sleep. But tonight, sleep would not find him.

CHAPTER 12

Aidan's Parents

Grandmama slowly opened the door into Aidan's room. It was early morning; the sun was just starting to rise. "Happy birthday, Aidan. I hope you slept..." To her surprise, she found him sitting straight up in his bed. "Whatever are you doing, boy? Why, look at those bags under your eyes! You look like you haven't slept a wink!"

"I couldn't sleep. There's something I need to ask you, something I should have asked you last night."

"Go on dear. You can ask me anything."

"I need to know if this prophecy and this journey I must take has anything to do with my parents."

"It has everything to do with your parents!" said Grandmama. "You are special because they were special."

"Tell me about them," pleaded Aidan. "I know so little."

Grandmama sat in a chair by Aidan's bed and looked squarely into his eyes. "I was wondering when this day would come, my precious Aidan. I think that you are old enough now to know right from wrong and understand the truth. Embrace it, although you will not yet completely understand it. I have often told you that your father is a very, very good man. But, he is much more than that. He was an important man who did many great things. Your father's name is Oren. The village in which you were raised bears his name."

"You've never told me about that!" said Aidan excitedly, rubbing his eyes.

"Oren had always wanted to be a healer. Even as a child he was drawn to the natural elements and how they could be used to heal disease. Many years ago, when Oren was a boy about your age, a plague fell upon the land. The guardians had already left, so there was no one to tell the people how to fight the plague. The sickness was very widespread. Even his father, Nolan, who was your grandfather and the love of my life, came down with the plague. Oren spent days without sleeping, desperately searching for an answer. The answer came from nature. He developed a cure for the disease from the bark of oak trees. He saved the village, which was renamed after him, but it was too late to save Nolan. Oren took the loss very hard, and vowed to never again let disease claim one that he loved. His interest in the elements became unquenchable. His studies of nature led him near and far. Eventually, he became much more than a healer, he became a powerful wizard."

"A wizard!" Aidan gasped.

"The story doesn't end there. As the years passed, Oren became so enraptured by nature, he created his mate from the very waters of Loch Myrror. He named her Belterra, because she came from the earth. They lived together for many years…so very happy…so very much in love. They conceived a child together. That child was you, Aidan."

"Grandmama, I can't believe this."

"Unfortunately, neither of them completely understood the greatest law of nature. The law of balance. What had started so beautifully ended in tragedy. It was not until your mother was close to delivering you that she and your father realized this most horrible truth: as a creature of nature, after creating you, Belterra had to return to nature."

"No! She must still be alive!"

"Aidan! If you are to know the truth, then you must be strong!" said Grandmama sternly. "Your mother would not want you to be sorrowful."

Aidan started to sob softly. "So I will never meet her?"

"That is not for me to say, my dear. Only time will tell."

Aidan could not talk, but he found comfort and strength in Grandmama's eyes.

"Do you understand now why the prophecy is about you? You are the child of Oren—unique in all of the world. You are half human and half natural. That is why the ground trembled when the hooded man reached for your friends." Grandmama leaned over and hugged Aidan tightly. "You cannot fathom your potential. This is why you must find and learn from the wise elves. They are natural creatures. You are connected to them in a very unique way. Don't be afraid."

Aidan of Oren

"I'll try to be brave, Grandmama," he said softly.

"Good. Remember Aidan, the world of the elves is elusive. According to the prophecy, you can only find them on the longest day of your thirteenth year—the summer soltice, which is a mere two days from today. Use the map to find your way to the Valley of the Elves. Your inner strength and natural abilities will help you find them once you are there."

Aidan's head was spinning.

"Gather your belongings, my child. It is time to go," Grandmama said as she left his room.

CHAPTER 13

Time to Go

As Grandmama prepared breakfast, Aidan began to gather a few belongings from his room for the journey. He looked at Charles, still fast asleep on his perch. Aidan chuckled as he thought of how Charles would react once he found out that they would be traveling to a place called the Dead Forest. He reached up and softly petted his old friend.

"Now, where did I put Lilly's necklace?" he said to himself. "And, where is that red stone Grandmama calls a dragon's scale?" He was trying to think quickly, but he was frustrated because he could not decide what to take with him. Also, his emotions were mixed; part of him was excited to explore the world around him, and part of him was sad. He truly loved his grandmama. Maybe she could go with them.

"No, my dear," she said as she peeked into his room. "I would only slow you down."

"But, I didn't even say anything..."

Grandmama winked over at him, "Hurry now, Lilly and McKenzie will soon be here."

"What?"

Aidan of Oren

"You weren't thinking of leaving without them, were you?"

"But, I hadn't even asked you yet."

"Aidan, as much as they need you, you need them. You cannot succeed without their help."

"But, what if something happens? What if I can't protect them?"

"You won't fail them, my child. The power of your bond is very strong. Don't forget that."

"Hello! Is anyone home?" Carl Kintz and his wife, Helfin, called from the front door.

"Quickly, Aidan, it's time," said Grandmama as she left the room. Aidan could hear the voices of Lilly and McKenzie as they entered the cottage. They seemed to be very excited. Aidan put on his cloak, and placed a sleepy Charles on his shoulder. He opened the door and looked around his room one last time, knowing that from this day forward his life would never be the same.

As Aidan entered the fireplace room, he saw Carl Kintz walking toward him. "Good morning," Carl said as he reached down and shook Aidan's hand. "Grandmama tells me that you are taking Lilly and McKenzie on a very important journey. They will be in your care now; I know that you will watch over them." Carl paused for a moment. "Your father would be very proud of you."

"Did you know him?" Aidan asked excitedly.

"Yes, we were very good friends. He had to leave when you were very young, but you will see him again one day."

Aidan's heart leaped inside of his chest. "I will? When, Mr. Kintz, when will I see him again?"

"When the time is right," smiled Carl as he put his arm around Aidan. "Until then, you must follow your own path."

McKenzie ran up and grabbed Aidan's arm. "We're really going with you!"

Lilly smiled at him from across the room. She beamed with confidence, which was reassuring to Aidan, who was still a little nervous about taking his best friends on a journey into the unknown. He glanced over at Helfin, who was staring right at him.

"You are wondering why we are allowing the girls to go with you. Am I right?" Helfin asked.

Aidan nodded.

"It might surprise you to learn that you are not the only child of destiny in this room." This got the immediate attention of Lilly and McKenzie. "Your destiny is entwined with theirs, as their destiny is with yours. Remember the prophecy? 'Wisdom, and a warrior, at his side?'"

Aidan glanced over at Lilly, his wise friend, and then down to McKenzie, his little warrior, beaming with confidence. The three children looked at each other in awkward amazement.

"I'll walk them to the edge of town," said Grandmama as she hugged Helfin and Carl. "Thank you both so much for all you've done."

As they turned to leave, Helfin reached for Aidan's shoulder and whispered in his ear, "He will be looking for you, Aidan. He knows you're coming. He and the one who sent him will do everything in their power to prevent you from fulfilling the prophecy, but you must! Or peace will be lost forever!"

"I know," said Aidan as he gave her a reassuring glance. "I know."

As they turned to walk home, Helfin reached over and took her husband's arm. "He has the courage of a lion, yes…and, by leaving most certainly has the spirit of the wind." She paused. "But, does he have the wisdom of a king?"

"Let us hope so…" said Carl. "The future of Lionsgate is in his hands."

The children followed Grandmama as she led them

toward the edge of town. Charles, who had awakened, was very agitated. "What's going on here? Why in blazes are we leaving? Where are we going?"

"We're going on a journey through the Dead Forest to the Valley of the Elves," said Aidan. "There's something we have to do, something very important. Just stay calm."

"Calm!" shrieked Charles. "You've got to be kidding! I'm not going to any sort of dead anything! Take me home!"

Grandmama gently reached up and stroked Charles' feathers, just behind his head. "It's going to be alright, Charles," she said softly. "Aidan needs you now. Everything's going to be alright." A great peace fell over Charles. He did not say another word.

Grandmama led the children up to the northern boundary of Oren, and stopped when they had come to the path called Sorrow's Way. She hugged Lilly and McKenzie tightly, and then turned to Aidan.

"For your journey," said Grandmama as she handed him Lilly's leather necklace, which now had the dragon scale attached to the end of it. "You don't want to forget this. Wear it around your neck for good luck."

Aidan of Oren

"Thank you, Grandmama. How did you…"

"Do you have the map?" Grandmama interrupted.

"Yes, I put it in my pouch."

"I have something else for you." She reached into her sack and pulled out something soft and started to unfold it. "For your birthday. This is a very special quilt, Aidan. Keep it with you always."

Aidan reached out and took the quilt from Grandmama. Holding it up to the light he gasped at the beauty of its design. Made of pure deep blue satin, the quilt had a curious emblem in the middle. It was strangely familiar to him, but he did not know why.

"What is this?"

"This quilt was made by your mother before you were born. She made it for you, Aidan. The emblem in the center represents the rising sun against the horizon."

"It's absolutely beautiful. Thank you, Grandmama," said Aidan as he hugged her tightly.

"You are the rising son, my child," said Grandmama as she released Aidan and stepped back. "Now, head north until you come to the base of Zorn Mountain, then head northwest through the Dead Forest and Woods of Didacus until you reach the Valley of the Elves. Your destiny awaits you there."

Grandmama continued, "Remember, you only have two days to journey to the Valley of the Elves. Do not allow yourself to be detained. Stay together and you will be safe."

Aidan of Oren

Lilly and McKenzie came up beside Aidan and each held one of his hands. Aidan mustered the bravest face he could, and gave his grandmama a hug goodbye. Placing a tender kiss on her cheek, he and the two girls turned to leave.

To the south was the entire village of Oren. He looked back one last time at Grandmama and the village where he had been raised. There was the village, but Grandmama was gone. Only the swirling of leaves could be seen. 'How could she…' but before he could complete the thought, he was met with a sudden breeze. "My love to you," he heard in the wind swirling all around him, "to all of you…my love."

To the South was the
Entire Village of Oren.

CHAPTER 14

The Journey Begins

The flowers were in full bloom, and a warm breeze blew in from the west. Aidan, with Charles on his shoulder, McKenzie, and Lilly, full of vigor and a good breakfast, started up the small path leading out of Oren to the north. The path, known as Sorrow's Way, wound through the Northern Forest, leading to the foothills of Zorn Mountain.

"What a beautiful day for an adventure," said McKenzie as she grinned from ear to ear.

"Quite an adventure it will be," agreed Lilly. "I'd say it just might be the adventure of a lifetime."

McKenzie started to talk faster. "How long until we get to the foothills of the mountain? What are we going to eat along the way? When will we…"

"Hold on, fireball," said Aidan, "one question at a time. The journey to the base of the mountain will take the better part of the day." Aidan stopped, looked up toward Zorn Mountain, and drew in a deep breath. "We should make it there safely if all goes well."

"What do you mean, if all goes well?" asked McKenzie. Lilly, who was walking just behind the other two, put her hand over her mouth in order to hide a growing smile.

"Aidan," persisted McKenzie, "what did you mean 'if all goes well'?"

"Oh, nothing. If we stay on the path we shouldn't run into the hooded man."

"The hooded man?!?" shrieked Charles. "We've got to turn back right away!" He buried his head deep into Aidan's neck and collar.

"The hooded man!" McKenzie said in a very loud whisper. "Don't worry, Charles, if we see him, I'll hit him with my stick!"

"Oh, McKenzie, it's no fun trying to scare you," said Aidan with a laugh. "Aren't you afraid of anything?"

"No," said Lilly, "she's a little warrior, you should know that by now. As for food, I've prepared something very special for the two of you." Charles, hearing the mention of food, quickly brought his head out of hiding.

"Oh, Lilly," said McKenzie, "did you make cream puffs again? Please say you did. Do you have them in your basket?"

"Don't you go anywhere without that thing?" asked Aidan, referring to the basket that Lilly had made for herself during the winter. Since finishing it, she had carried it everywhere.

"It's very much like the pouch you carry over your shoulder," said Lilly. "Except I don't use it to carry around creepy bugs and slimy turtles."

"So, Lilly, do you have any goodies in your basket

for me?" asked Charles.

"Well, if I don't, I'm sure that Aidan will have something in his shoulder pouch for you."

"That's not funny," quipped Charles. "I have a very sensitive stomach!"

The meadowlands soon turned into woodlands as the four of them ventured into the Northern Forest.

"Why is this path called Sorrow's Way?" asked McKenzie.

"They say the mountain is sad," said Aidan. "There is a fable about how once there were two majestic mountains that stood here—one was named Zorn and the other was named Zir. There they stood, side by side, for thousands of years, together touching the sky. Until one day, a great dragon arose from the Ring of Fire and smote one of the mountains, leveling it into barren wasteland."

"That must have been Zir," whispered McKenzie.

"That's right," said Aidan, "and ever since that day, Zorn weeps for his lost companion. It is said that there is a great river that begins at the base of the mountain. It is called the River of Tears."

"That is a very sad story," said Lilly. "Do you really think that mountains have feelings?"

"I don't know," said Aidan soberly, as he led them deeper into the Northern Forest. The canopy from the thick trees provided welcome shade for the explorers.

"I'm hungry," McKenzie whimpered. "Can we stop now?"

"Not yet," said Aidan. "It's almost midday, and we haven't made very good time. I'd like to get to the base

The Journey Begins

ONE DAY A GREAT DRAGON AROSE AND SMOTE ONE OF THE MONTAINS

of the mountain while it's still daylight. I've heard of a Great Sitting Rock found there…I'm anxious to see it."

"A sitting rock?" asked Lilly. "What could that possibly be?"

"It is a rock where you go to think," said Aidan.

"What do you think about on the sitting rock, Aidan?" asked McKenzie. Then she giggled. "Maybe, if it's a big rock, you might think about how you're going to get down!"

"Don't be silly, McKenzie," said Aidan. "A sitting rock is where you go to think deep thoughts."

"Oooohhh, deep thoughts," smirked Lilly.

"If I knew the two of you were going to tease me the whole way, I'd have left without you!" he joked. "Look, we're not even halfway there, and you're already…"

All of a sudden Charles popped his head out from Aidan's collar. "Aidan! Did you hear that?"

CHAPTER 15

The Trolls

T he three children stopped and listened intently. They heard nothing. Aidan turned to notice that the falcon's eyes were wide open with sheer fright.

"Charles, there's nothing out here."

"Aidan, Lilly, and McKenzie," Charles said slowly, yet with great trembling, "you must leave this place immediately."

Lilly grabbed Aidan's arm. "What is he talking about?"

"Charles! Tell us what you heard!" insisted Aidan. But Charles could no longer talk.

Lilly clutched Aidan tighter. "What's wrong with him?"

"I'm not sure."

"It's not what he heard," interrupted McKenzie, "it's what he didn't hear."

Aidan stopped to listen again. "Lilly," he said slowly, "we're in the middle of a forest, and there are no sounds."

"What does that mean?" she asked, as her trembling hand covered her mouth.

"It means," said McKenzie, "that something's out here

with us. Something so dreadful, everything else in this part of the forest is now gone."

"Trolls!" said Aidan.

"Two of them are directly in front of us, around those trees," whispered McKenzie. "At least one is behind us and there are more on either side of us. We're surrounded."

"How do you know this?" asked Lilly nervously.

"I'm shorter than you," said McKenzie calmly. "I'm looking them right in the eye."

Aidan looked around, this time lower to the ground. He spotted two trolls hiding behind some nearby shrubs. They were short and thick, with hideous faces and grotesquely crooked teeth. Their skin was very dark, and they had wild hair on their misshapen heads. Their hands were thick and strong.

"We need to stay calm," he said as he backed up toward Lilly and McKenzie. "Maybe if we make a run for it…"

It was too late. A troll grabbed Lilly by the ankles, and she fell to the ground. The troll was pulling her into the trees.

"Aidan!" she screamed. "Do something!"

"Use the wish poem," said McKenzie. She was staring straight ahead, a troll locked in her sight. "Quickly, Aidan. Before it's too late."

A pair of trolls grabbed Aidan, one firmly holding onto each of his arms. They started pulling him away. "What do you mean?" he screamed.

The Trolls

Aidan of Oren

McKenzie's eyes began to roll back in her head as the troll's stare became stronger. "Hurry, Aidan…" she said weakly. "Hurry!"

Lilly had stopped screaming. Aidan saw her sitting by a tree; a troll was standing in front of her. She was locked in its gaze, and her life was slowly being drained from her. He looked back at McKenzie, who was now completely helpless. Aidan's heart was stirred. Courage replaced what was once fear, and suddenly he knew what he must do. He had to take a leap of faith. He shook his right arm free from one of the trolls and flung himself to the ground.

"**Make a little wish**," he said, as he closed his eyes and wished with all of his might.

"**Hold it in your hand**," he continued, stretching his closed hand out in front of him.

"**Kneel to the ground, and rub it in the sand.**"

The Trolls

He rose to a knee and rubbed his hand down into the dirt. He was oblivious to the trolls around him, trying frantically to pull him away, and trying to catch his gaze.

"**Look up to the heavens, and there pronounce your name.**" He raised his head toward the sky and shouted, "I am Aidan of Oren!"

"**The wind will grant your wish,**" he said softly,

"**But you'll never be the same,**" he finished, with his eyes closed reverently.

Thunder rolled through the valley. A great wind started to blow, and the ground shook mightily, as if the very elements had hastened to his bidding. And then there was silence. Aidan slowly opened his eyes. The two trolls that had tried to abduct him now lay beside him, lifeless and still. He stood up and looked around.

"Lilly! McKenzie! Where are you?" he shouted, still a bit dazed.

"We're right here, Aidan," came Lilly's soft voice from behind him. She had McKenzie by the hand. Both seemed to be a bit rattled, but otherwise they were fine. "What happened? There was a great thunder, and then, well, all of the trolls, they fell to the ground."

"It was the wish poem, wasn't it?" asked McKenzie, taking hold of Aidan's hand.

Aidan stood in silence. As he looked around, he saw the trolls that had attacked them were indeed dead. He tried to justify what had happened. Trolls were horrible, dangerous creatures who threatened their lives. Still, he felt a deep sadness.

Aidan of Oren

The wish poem was right—he would never be the same.

CHAPTER 16

Tears of Zorn

Aidan composed himself and drew a deep breath. "Are both of you alright?"

"We're fine, Aidan," said Lilly as she looked around. "However, our belongings seem to be scattered all about. It will take a while to gather our things." She picked up her basket and started searching.

Aidan knelt down beside McKenzie and looked at her. He slowly raised his hand and moved aside the few strands of beautiful golden hair that lay in front of her face. In those blue, piercing eyes he saw strength beyond her years. Throughout this frightful ordeal, she never panicked. But how had she known what he had to do?

"How did you know that I should use the elf poem? How did you know that it would even work?"

A tiny smile crept across McKenzie's face. "Because you are Aidan of Oren," she said softly. "I have heard the elves talk about you."

Aidan stepped back, startled. "What do you mean, they talk about me? What did they say?"

"Well, I haven't sat down to tea with them or anything. I've just heard them down in your well, singing and talking in rhymes. They say that you are natural."

"Natural?" asked Aidan.

"I don't know," said McKenzie lightly. "It's just what they say, that's all. I don't think it's anything to worry about."

Aidan thought about what Grandmama had said regarding his mother. She was a creature of nature. Is this what the elves meant by referring to him as natural? Aidan looked around. "Has anyone seen Charles?"

Aidan got no response, other than blank expressions. In all of the excitement, Charles seemed to have been forgotten. They immediately started to look for him. Lilly and McKenzie traced their steps back down Sorrow's Way while Aidan walked just off of the path, where the forest undergrowth was very thick. It was full of thorny plants, many taller than Aidan, which made walking very slow and difficult. They looked for quite a while before Aidan's foot bumped into something. He cleared away the plants to get a better look.

Aidan glanced over at his two friends. Once he had made eye contact with them, he put his finger over his lips. Then, he motioned for them to quietly hurry over.

"What is it?" whispered McKenzie as she and Lilly came closer.

"Shhhh!" he said, trying to keep things as quiet as possible. He motioned downward with his right hand, as he gently pulled the brush aside with his left. There, at the base of a tree with his head wedged tightly in a hole, was Charles.

"Do you think he's stuck in there?" whisperd Lilly.

"No," Aidan whispered back, "I think he's hiding."

"Let's scare him," said McKenzie, trying her best to hold back laughter.

"I don't know if that's such a good idea," whispered Aidan. "He's been through a lot." Then, with a mischievous look in his eye, he said, "Oh, why not!" He leaned toward Charles, and yelled, "The trolls are coming!"

"AAAHHHH!!!" shrieked Charles as his two little feet raced desperately to wedge his head into the hole even tighter. "They're going to eat me!"

All three of the children laughed. Charles became immediately silent. He slowly backed out of the hole, stood up as straight as he possibly could, and looked up at Aidan.

"That's not funny, you know," he said in a dry voice. "However, I am pleased to see that you are all doing well, even if it is at my expense. I was just looking for you, you know."

"Well, you're not going to find us in that hole!" laughed Lilly.

"Hmmph," Charles mumbled. "But, what happened to the trolls? I fell off Aidan's shoulder when two of the awful beasts grabbed him." Charles paused for a moment and collected himself. "I could not bear to watch any further. How did you escape?"

"Aidan called for the wind to steal their breath away," answered McKenzie. "He used the wish poem to call on the wind to destroy the trolls, and the wind answered him."

Aidan didn't say a word. He knew that McKenzie's words were true.

"McKenzie," asked Lilly. "Are you saying that the wish poem is magical?"

"I don't think it would work for you and me," she replied quite candidly, "just for Aidan, because he's natural."

"Natural?"

"Don't ask," interrupted Aidan. "I'm not sure if I understand it either." He drew a deep breath. "What I do understand is that we need to get moving if we want to reach the base of Zorn Mountain before darkness falls."

"Yes," agreed Charles lightheartedly, "we must be on our way. And, if we're lucky, maybe we'll chance upon some mystical elves, or maybe some purple dancing puppies, or maybe even some flying kitties!"

"Charles!" scolded McKenzie. "There are no such things as purple dancing puppies and flying kitties!"

"And," added Charles, "there's no such thing as elves or a silly wish poem."

"Why, certainly there are!"

"Alrighty then!" mocked Charles. "Maybe we'll just pop in on them for a surprise visit."

"We can't surprise them." McKenzie looked Charles right in the eye. "They already know we're coming."

"Wait, I hear something," hushed Aidan, stopping suddenly. "Do you hear that?"

The others stopped walking and listened.

Tears of Zorn

"It sounds like thunder, but off in the distance," said Lilly.

"Oh, no!" cried Charles. "It's probably a monster. We should leave this dreadful place immediately!"

"Wait, I see something," shouted McKenzie as she took off running.

"No!" yelled Aidan as he started running after her. "Stay with us!"

When he caught up to McKenzie, she was standing on the bank of a very wide river. Lilly came to a stop beside him, and all they could do was murmur a soft "ahhhh" as they beheld the river's splendor.

"I've never seen anything like it," said Aidan. "You can see clear to the bottom. And, look at those fish; they are *huge*!"

"Look at the trees rooted in the bank of the river," said Lilly. "Their trunks are broad, and their branches majestic, and, look higher! Look at all of the birds!" Then her excitement turned to a whisper. "But, with so many birds, why is there no sound?"

"Maybe this is a sanctuary," whispered Aidan.

McKenzie tugged at his tunic. "This is the River of Tears."

"I don't know… let me check the map," Aidan said as he unrolled the scroll. "Yes, we should follow along the bank of the river."

Charles buried his head in Aidan's collar and mumbled, "I don't think we should be here."

They continued to walk down the bank in silence. The thunder they had heard off in the distance was getting closer. The river turned sharply to the left, and the forest ended, giving way to twin waterfalls, each jutting out of rocky caverns forming the base of the mountain. The waterfalls poured toward each other and exploded onto a massive pile of boulders, creating an eerie mist.

Aidan swallowed hard, and in a very solemn voice said, "the tears of Zorn."

The tears of Zorn

CHAPTER 17

Kartha

idan stood at the base of the twin waterfalls, staring upward in utter awe and amazement. The mist, which he found cool and refreshing, was generated by the tremendous amount of water crashing down onto a giant pile of rocks in front of him.

"The River of Tears begins here," he said to no one in particular. "It's almost as if you can feel the deep and desperate sadness of the mountain, cursed to weep for its lost companion forever more. Standing here, I know that the mountain is sad. I don't know how I know this, but I do."

"I believe you," said McKenzie. "But, could a dragon really destroy a whole mountain?" Aidan did not reply.

"Aidan, perhaps we should make camp and prepare the food," said Lilly. "This clearing by the waterfall should work perfectly, and we can use that large rock over by the trees as a table."

"Yes, good thinking," replied Aidan, as he regained his bearings.

Charles raised his head from Aidan's collar. "Food? Did someone say food?"

Kartha

Aidan and McKenzie helped Lilly spread out a blanket on a large rock and unpack. While Lilly began to set out the meal she had prepared, Aidan noticed McKenzie venturing down toward the bank of the river.

"Don't wander off, McKenzie," said Aidan as he went after her, "I don't want to lose you in the mist."

"I don't like this place," quivered Charles, "can we leave now?"

Aidan started to reply when he noticed McKenzie sitting on the ground, taking her shoes off. "What are you doing?"

"I'm going to step into the river, silly, and I don't want to get my shoes wet."

"I don't know if that's a wise thing to do," cautioned Aidan. "This is a strange place, and we don't really know what's in the water."

"Look at all the fish in there!" giggled McKenzie. "I can see them right through the clear water, and it's very shallow here. I won't go in past my knees." McKenzie tossed her shoes aside and splashed into the river. "Oooh, the water feels so good! You should join me!"

"Well, as long as the water is clear and shallow, maybe just for a little bit."

"No!" yelled Charles. "Not with me on your shoulder! Please put me down and I'll walk back to camp to supervise the meal preparations. I can protect Lilly while the two of you frolic about."

"Why don't you just fly back, oh mighty protector?" asked Aidan as he placed Charles on the ground.

"That's not funny," sneered Charles.

Indeed, it was not funny. Aidan had found Charles a few years earlier at the base of a tree. The baby falcon had fallen out of its nest and was helpless. Aidan took him home, to nurture and raised him. To this day, Charles had never even attempted to fly.

"I'm sorry, Charles. But, you know, you're going to have to try to fly one of these days. That's just what birds do."

"You should not refer to me as a mere bird," quipped Charles. "I am a regal falcon…"

"…from the royal family of Wingdom," said McKenzie with a giggle.

"Hmphh!" snorted Charles, and he abruptly turned around, heading toward the clearing to join Lilly.

Kartha

Aidan slipped off his shoes and walked slowly into the river to join McKenzie. The water felt pleasantly cool and silky to the touch. Velvety soft sand lined the river bottom. He watched with amusement as McKenzie darted back and forth, trying to catch a fish. The river was very shallow at this end, and certainly seemed safe.

"What are you going to do with the fish once you catch him?" Aidan asked.

"I'm going to eat him!" said McKenzie defiantly. "I'll take him back for Lilly to cook, and I'm going to eat him all up!"

Aidan smiled at his little friend. "If you really want to catch him, you'll need a long stick, with a bit of string and a net. You take the string and…"

"Got him!" McKenzie proudly pulled a bright yellow fish from the river.

"What? How did you do that?"

"I just squeezed my hands together and I got him! I got him, and now I'm going to…" McKenzie brought the fish to her face. She stood there for a moment looking deeply into its eyes. Her face went pale.

"What's wrong, McKenzie? Did that fish just bite you?"

"No," whispered McKenzie. "We were just talking. He told me that his name was Bernard, and that it was all right if we wanted to eat him. But, he wants us to know that we need to get out of the water immediately!"

MCKENZIE STARED INTO THE EYES of the FISH

Kartha

A chill went down Aidan's spine as he looked around in the water. It was not clear like before. Rather it was beginning to cloud up and turn red. Aidan quickly snatched McKenzie out of the river and started carrying her back toward the riverbank. He heard a great churning noise coming down the river toward them. The water bubbled and frothed. Aidan could feel countless fish bumping into his legs, desperately trying to get downstream; trying to get away.

"Almost there!" gasped Aidan as he tossed McKenzie onto the riverbank. Suddenly, a giant water snake with a massive set of fangs lurched out of the water toward Aidan, grabbed his right foot and pulled him out into the middle of the river. McKenzie screamed from the bank of the river as she saw the monster drag Aidan under the water.

Aidan frantically twisted and turned with all of his might until he broke free from the snake's grip. He gasped for air as he reached the surface, and clamored up onto the dry riverbank. He turned toward the river, and watched in horror as the great snake swam over to the bank and raised its head out of the water, facing him.

"How did you know I wasssss coming?" it hissed.

Keeping his gaze directly on the snake, Aidan backed up on the bank. The creature was unlike anything Aidan had ever seen. From its size, Aidan deduced it to be more of a sea serpent than a water snake. It was black as midnight, and made a horrible hissing sound. Its evil eyes were fixed on Aidan.

Aidan of Oren

STARTLED, HE TWISTED AND TURNED

Kartha

"Who are you?" Aidan mustered. The great serpent stared intently at him.

"I am Kartha!" it hissed, now with its head starting to move slightly side to side. "And I know who you are, Aidan of Oren!" The deadly serpent hissed again and began to move up onto the bank. Suddenly, it stopped and looked up at McKenzie, who was now standing defiantly over Aidan. "Isssss she going to protect you from me?" The great serpent began to laugh hideously.

Aidan looked over toward the waterfall. "How long can you stay out of the water, Kartha?" he asked.

"Long enough to take care of you!"

"We will see about that…" Even before Aidan could complete his sentence, they were all overcome with a deafening silence. The great waterfall had suddenly stopped. Without its continuous supply of water, the River of Tears quickly began to dry up.

"What?" exclaimed Kartha. "No!" The great snake quickly headed back to what little water was left, swimming downstream with all of its might in order to avoid certain death.

McKenzie moved over to sit beside Aidan. "What was that creature? How did it know your name?"

Aidan was silent.

"Did you stop the waterfall?"

Again, Aidan said nothing.

"Are you alright? Say something."

"That was close," he said soberly as he collected himself. "I knew that the water was going to stop…but how?" At that moment, the twin waterfalls were suddenly restored. Water again crashed to the boulders below, replenishing the river. Aidan looked curiously over at McKenzie. "Why are you still holding onto that fish?"

"His name is Bernard! You didn't think I'd put him back in the water with that awful snake, did you?"

"Of course not. I understand, you didn't want to lose out on a tasty fish dinner."

McKenzie looked up with disgust. "We're certainly not going to eat him after he saved our lives."

"Oh, that's right, the fish told you that we were in danger!"

McKenzie looked down at the fish still clutched in her little hands. "You're mocking me," she said softly. "Bernard told me we were in danger, and we were, weren't we?"

Aidan softened his tone. "It's just that I didn't hear anything, and I was standing right beside you."

"I heard him in my head."

Aidan had to admit to himself that something was strange about this fish, which did not seem to mind being out of the water. Maybe it was a special, magical fish. But, Grandmama's stories did not mention such a creature.

Aidan put his hand on McKenzie's head. "I believe you. It's just a shame that, well, he's such a wonderful fish and all, but we do need food for the long journey. It's just too bad we're going to have to eat him anyway."

"No!" shouted McKenzie. "Bernard saved us. We should let him go."

"I was just kidding! We'll let him go. But do you really think he wants to go back into the river with that horrible snake?"

McKenzie stared into the eyes of the fish. "Bernard says it's alright now, the danger is gone." She walked down to the bank of the river and gently placed the fish back into the water and let it go. The fish hovered for a moment in the spot where it was placed, and then swam in a small circle facing McKenzie. It stopped for a moment, as if to say goodbye, and then continued to swim downstream and out of their sight.

Aidan and McKenzie returned to the clearing where Lilly had prepared a great meal. As they ate, they told of their harrowing adventure in the river. They all laughed, except for Charles, who had just finished his cream puff and was walking away.

"What's wrong, Charles?" asked Aidan. "Aren't these stories incredible?"

"Incredible?" smirked the falcon. "Disappearing mountains, emotional rivers, vampire water snakes, and a telepathic fish. I'd say the stories are a bit more than just incredible and your imaginations are beginning to get the best of you!" Charles found a small tree where, using his claws and his beak, he climbed to the lowest perch. Glancing back at Aidan one more time, Charles managed to utter a slight "hmmph!" He stuck his beak into his back feathers and prepared to take a nap.

CHAPTER 18

The Dead Forest

illy and Aidan cleaned up the remnants from their meal and began to set up camp for the night. As Lilly turned for her basket, she was startled to find McKenzie had been standing right behind her. McKenzie's eyes were wide open.

"McKenzie!" exclaimed Lilly. "Don't sneak up on us like that, it's not funny!" McKenzie just stood there, as if she was staring right through Lilly. "What's wrong?"

"The trees are coming to get us. They have big claws. I can see them moving."

"Stop teasing," said Lilly. "This is no time for playing any of your foolish games."

"I don't think she is playing," said Aidan. The wind whipped around them as they huddled together at the edge of the forest. "Have you noticed that these trees don't have any leaves?" he whispered. "Their bare branches stretch forward like giant arms."

"Are they going to eat us?" McKenzie asked, her voice shaking.

"I don't think so, but they do look hungry, don't they?" McKenzie turned and playfully kicked at Aidan.

"We might be standing at the edge of the Dead Forest. It is said that the Great Sitting Rock guards the entrance into that forest. But, I don't see any Great Sitting Rock."

"What about this one?" asked McKenzie, pointing to the rock they had used as a table. "Maybe this is the Great Sitting Rock."

Aidan laughed. "I don't think so. The Great Sitting Rock is just that: a great rock. I'm sure that it's over ten feet tall. This one is small. Look, it doesn't even come up to my waist! Why, if it were any smaller I could use it in a game of marbles!"

"We need to finish setting up camp," said Lilly. "It's starting to get dark. But, where's Charles?"

The Dead Forest

Aidan cupped his hands around his mouth and yelled "Charles!" into the woods, but there was no answer. "Charles!"

The Dead Forest offered only silence.

"You don't think the trees got him, do you?" whispered McKenzie.

"Could be, but one would think that they would soon grow tired of him and beg us to take him home."

"I heard that!" said Charles as he walked out of the woods. "Go ahead, make fun, but I found something very interesting in that forest."

"You found something in the Dead Forest?" Lilly and McKenzie said together in horror.

"Dead Forest!" Charles shrieked as he ran over to Aidan. "What do you mean Dead Forest? Aidan! Don't just stand there, pick me up at once!"

"Don't worry," he said as he reached down for his feathered friend. "I'm sure the forest's bark is worse than its bite."

McKenzie and Lilly groaned.

As the sun went down, the children built a small fire and sat in a circle around it. In the cool evening air, the warmth from the fire felt good.

"It was quite a day," said Aidan, as he lifted his left shoe up in front of him. A hole had worn through the tip, revealing one wiggly toe.

"You're just lucky the snake didn't get that juicy toe," laughed Lilly.

"I don't know what you're laughing about," quipped Charles. "If the situation was really as bad as you say it was, you wouldn't be making a jolly ho-ho of it now!"

"His name was Kartha," added McKenzie. "Lucky for him I was holding Bernard and not my stick!" Everyone laughed, except Charles.

"Oh, Charles," said Aidan, "you need to lighten up a little. What happened cannot be changed. Better to make light of it than to fret."

"Make light of the situation?" exclaimed Charles. "Tell me this, just how did he know your name?"

"I don't know. I'm still a bit confused about the whole thing."

Charles puffed out his chest. "Well then, it's a good thing that one of us is mature enough to see that something's just not right here!"

Aidan reached up and rubbed the back of Charles' neck. Not only did it show appreciation to his feathered friend, it also served another purpose; putting the falcon to sleep.

"Maybe Charles has a point," said Lilly. "Maybe the hooded man or whoever sent him is trying to stop you from fulfilling your destiny."

"I'll admit, something about this doesn't feel right,"

said Aidan. "But, we may just have to chalk it up to a mystery for now. Speaking of which, I believe I know of another mystery that has been solved!"

"I hear a story coming!" squealed McKenzie.

"What kind of mystery?" asked Lilly. "Is this another of your fantasy stories?"

"Actually, this one's real." He reached for his necklace. "Remember this?"

"That's the pretty rock I found for you!" exclaimed McKenzie. Lilly nodded in agreement.

"Well, last night, Grandmama told me that the rock we found wasn't even a rock at all…it's a dragon scale!"

"Dragons?" said Lilly. "That's incredible!"

"That's not all," said Aidan. "Grandmama says that the guardians we've heard about were actually dragons. They are the ones that used to live with us and help us make the laws. We have to find them so that the land can be at peace once more."

"No wonder the Hall of Judges was so big," said McKenzie.

"That's right," said Aidan. "The elves are the only ones who know where the guardians are. They're going to teach us about the dragons."

"I want to catch a dragon!" exclaimed McKenzie. "What an adventure that would be!"

CHAPTER 19

Ring of Fire

Which way shall we go in the morning?" asked Lilly.

"Well," said Aidan, "we're at the base of Zorn Mountain. If we continue northwest through those trees, we'll be heading directly for the Valley of the Elves."

"Valley of the Elves!" echoed McKenzie.

"Helfin spoke of this place," said Lilly, "but quite honestly, we really didn't know what she was talking about."

"She said that we're special," interrupted McKenzie. "She said that somebody wrote a story about us a long time ago."

Lilly shrugged her shoulders. "Like I said, we really didn't quite understand what she was saying, only that it was important that we go with you and help you find the elves. But how will we know where they are?"

Aidan reached for his pouch. He opened the top flap and pulled out the map Grandmama had given him.

"Here," Aidan said, handing over the map. "See for yourself."

"The map!" exclaimed McKenzie and Lilly together.

"Hold on, you two. I haven't really had a chance to study it."

"Let's study it together!" said Lilly.

"Maybe it's a treasure map!" squealed McKenzie. "Do you suppose there's treasure to be found?"

Aidan held the map up in the light of the fire. "The map itself is a treasure. It reveals places and lands that we've never even dreamed of."

McKenzie was fidgeting, trying to get in a position to better view the map. She pointed toward the left side of the parchment and said, "What's that curious circle?"

"Do you see these little symbols here?" explained Aidan. "These are mountains." Aidan pointed as he referenced different locations. "Here is Oren, and this curved line heading up from there is Sorrow's Way. That's the path we took today."

"That must be Zorn Mountain," McKenzie said, as she pointed to the map. "It sure is smaller on the map than in real life."

"It's a good thing, too," joked Aidan, "or else it would be very difficult to carry around."

"But, what about that circle over here?" said McKenzie, again pointing to the curious markings on the map. "Those don't look like mountains, not like Zorn Mountain."

"She's right," said Lilly, "there is something a little different about that circle…"

Aidan took a closer look at the map. It was true, the mountains forming a circle looked a little different than the rest of the mountains on the map. They seemed to be cut off at the top.

"Volcanoes!" Lilly said, "forming a circle…the Ring of Fire!"

"Ooooohhhhh, the Ring of Fire," McKenzie echoed. "But, isn't that supposed to be a very bad place?"

Grandmama had told stories about the Ring of Fire. It was a place of darkness and mystery. No one who had ever traveled into that land had ever returned.

"Hmmm…I think we'll just stick to finding the elves," said Aidan.

"I want to see the dragons!" pouted McKenzie. Then she brightened up. "But at least we'll get to show smarty pants Charles that elves really exist!"

"Let's get some sleep," said Lilly. "We'll take one day at a time."

Aidan knew Lilly was right. It would be best to rest tonight, and let some decisions take care of themselves. He watched as she helped McKenzie find a comfortable spot to sleep, and was touched as she kissed McKenzie goodnight on the forehead. She checked the fire one last time for the night, and walked over to sit beside Aidan.

"Can I take another look at the map?" she asked quietly.

Aidan positioned the map so that both of them could see it clearly against the firelight. Lilly pointed first to Oren, and then up to Zorn Mountain. She slowly moved her hand to the far right side of the map, her finger stopping where the land formed a great gulf, meeting the sea.

Ring of Fire

"This is Land's End. This is where I was born."

"How do you know? You came to Oren when you were just a baby."

"I wasn't that young, Aidan. I remember the wind blowing in off of the sea, and the pure white sand." Lilly pointed to the blue portions of the map, which represented the sea. "There are islands out here. They don't show on the map, but they're there. I remember being taken out in the fishing boats."

"Do you want to go back there?"

"Maybe someday." Lilly rolled up the map and put it back into Aidan's pouch. "But not now. This quest is not for me, Aidan. It is for you, and all of Lionsgate."

McKenzie stirred, and then started snoring. Aidan and Lilly looked at each other and laughed.

CHAPTER 20

The Great Sitting Rock

he summer night air was surprisingly cool. Lilly soon fell fast asleep next to McKenzie. Aidan lay nearby, staring at the night sky. The moon had never looked so large, nor the stars so bright. The stars seemed to dance through the heavens with such beauty, such precision, as if guided by a great, unseen hand. The fire had burned down to embers giving off a soft, warm glow. All was quiet except for the soothing sound of the waterfall.

Although he joked about the danger they avoided earlier in the day, deep down Aidan worried about his ability to protect his friends.

As he traced their path on the map through the Dead Forest, he thought about the Valley of the Elves. It made him shudder to think that the Ring of Fire was a real place. The Plain of Zir didn't have much more to offer, either. From the stories he had heard, this was a place of great desolation. How could he expose Lilly and McKenzie to this type of danger? And just what would they find inside the Dead Forest?

He stared intently into the sky, but he found no answers there. As sleep would not come, Aidan stood up, brushed off the dirt, and looked tenderly at Lilly and McKenzie, sleeping at the base of a tree.

"I will take care of you," he said softly. "With my very life, I will take care of you."

Aidan walked off across the clearing, coming to the edge of the Dead Forest. In the moonlight, the trees without leaves were indeed unsettling. He could hear a soft breeze whistling through their branches as they gently swayed from side to side.

This was a place of great mystery. Although the trees bore no leaves, they were not truly dead. The legend of the Dead Forest was linked directly to the stories of Zir Mountain. Long ago, when the great and terrible dragon laid waste to the mountain, the forest at the base of Zir quickly abandoned its leaves in the hope that the great dragon would believe it too had also been destroyed. The plan worked, but not without its consequences. In nature, a forest that abandons its leaves can never call them back.

There, at the edge of the forest, was the rock on which they dined. He looked up to the sky and said, "Who are you, Aidan of Oren? Who are you to think that you're ready for what lies ahead?"

He paused. It felt good to speak aloud and ask these questions. He was far enough away from where the girls slept that they could not hear him. His spirit grew bolder as he stood taller and pointed over to the trees. "And who are you, oh forest of old, to stand here content? You have seen the past. You alone know why your leaves

Aidan of Oren

"With my very Life, I will take Care of you"

deny you."

Aidan could not believe the words coming out of his mouth. Something about these words felt right, even though he was not quite sure why he was saying them. His heart was racing, and he could not stop.

"I bid you, oh great forest, to make amends with those that you have long since cast aside. For that which once was can be again."

Aidan was now breathing harder, and sweat began to form on his brow. He walked over to the rock where they had eaten their meal. "Who are you, oh simple rock? Who are you to say nothing? You have seen the past, and you have beheld the great mystery. How many generations more will you live in total silence?"

Completely out of breath, Aidan sat on the ground. His legs were trembling. Suddenly, the ground rumbled beneath him, and the wind blew violently through the trees. And then, all became quiet.

Aidan heard a sound, like two great grinding stones rolling together.

"How many generations have gone by, how many years have I waited, with no one to talk to..."

Aidan was startled. "Who said that?" he asked, mustering all of the courage within him.

"My name is Grock."

Although the voice was very large, it was not frightening.

**"I am the keeper of wisdom.
I am the keeper of knowledge.**

Aidan of Oren

BEWARE, AIDEN of OREN

I am the keeper of this land."

The light from the moon and stars was enough for Aidan to see that the rock was slowly sliding toward him. Aidan gasped as he saw that the rock had formed a face with eyes and a mouth.

"Am I dreaming?" Aidan asked as he jumped to his feet.

**"As a boy you dreamed.
You are a boy no longer."**

"So, I'm not dreaming," said Aidan.

**"You have summoned me, Aidan of Oren.
What is it that you would know?"**

Aidan, trying his best not to show his fear, thought about what he had said earlier... 'who are you to be silent.' Then he remembered a story his Grandmama had told about the Great Sitting Rock being a creature of great wisdom and understanding. A creature who was the keeper of the land.

"Are you the Great Sitting Rock?" asked Aidan.

"It is as you have said. My name is Grock."

"You are not how I imagined you would be," admitted Aidan. "I thought you would be much larger, with a majestic sitting place for one to think. I had pictured you more like a king's throne."

"Beware, Aidan of Oren,
the mind's eye is easily deceived.
Seek the inner beauty.
What is it that you would know?"

A sense of excitement rushed through Aidan's veins. He had so many questions, but where would he start? Should he ask about elves or about dragons? What about the Ring of Fire?

Then, just before the very first words could pass through his lips, he stopped. He took a step back and looked at the Great Sitting Rock. It was so plain, so simple and ordinary. Aidan's mind became clear.

"I wish to know wisdom," he said softly. "We have set out on a journey into the great unknown. Therefore, grant me wisdom, so that I might know how to keep my companions from harm."

"Aidan of Oren,
a request from the heart
is a request granted.
The beginning of wisdom is understanding.
Therefore, listen not with your ears,
But with your heart."

Then there was silence. The wind had stopped and Aidan could hear nothing but the steady rumbling of the waterfall in the background. Deep sorrow filled his soul as he listened.

Grock again began to speak.

"Zorn mourns for her,
his tears will forever flow.
But in death, there is life.
What once was lost will soon be found.
A ray of light to pierce the darkness.
There will be hope for the hopeless."

Aidan was filled with awe. "So, the mountain called Zir really did exist."

"For eons she reached for the sky.
Until, from the belly of the earth,
the great beast came and smote her."

"You mean a great dragon?"

"Not a dragon.
A destroyer of dragons."

"Grock," asked Aidan, "how do these words help me? How do I protect those in my care? How will I know the correct path to take?"

"The beginning of wisdom is understanding.
Do not fret for your path,
for your path will find you."

"What does that mean?" Aidan asked excitedly. But there was no answer. "Grock, my quest is to find the elves. Can you help me?"

Again, there was no answer. Grock had gone silent. Aidan stood before the Great Sitting Rock for what seemed like a very long time.

"Please, Grock, speak to me again," he begged. "There is still so much I don't understand. You haven't told me how to protect my friends. You haven't told me how to find the elves."

To Aidan's dismay, Grock did not respond. Aidan returned to the campsite in the middle of the clearing with mixed feelings. He lay back on his quilt, now very tired and confused. His friends were sleeping peacefully. What would they think of all this? Would they believe him? As his eyes grew heavier, he wondered if he even believed it himself.

CHAPTER 21

Diamonds

idan was awakened by a shuffling beside him. He quickly sat up and saw his quilt bobbing around as if it had a life of its own. "What are you doing under there, Charles, trying to make off with my quilt?" he asked. The mist was heavy that morning. He noticed that Lilly and McKenzie were already up and standing off in the clearing.

"Aidan!" yelled McKenzie, "we didn't want to wake you, but there's something that you have got to see!"

Aidan rubbed his eyes and looked out in the direction McKenzie was pointing. Through the mist, all he could see was Lilly standing with her back to the both of them.

"Aidan, you're not seeing it! Look out there, past Lilly!"

Walking over to McKenzie, Aidan looked harder. There was Lilly, still with her back to them. "What is she looking at?" asked Aidan, growing concerned.

McKenzie grabbed Aidan's hand and started pulling him over to where Lilly was standing. "You're not seeing it! Come closer!"

Diamonds

"Do you see it?" asked Lilly as they walked up behind her.

Aidan looked out through the mist toward the Dead Forest. Astonished by what he saw, Aidan again rubbed his eyes. "What…?"

"It's the most beautiful thing I've ever seen!" said Lilly.

"They look like diamonds!" whispered McKenzie.

Aidan stared into the Dead Forest. He was speechless. He couldn't believe he hadn't noticed it before. Every tree, every branch on every tree, and all of the branches stemming off of all of the branches had sprung to life. New buds were everywhere. In the early mist, they bore the appearance of millions of tiny diamonds suspended in the air.

Aidan remembered back to the night before and the words that had come out of his mouth.

"For that which once was can be again."

"The Dead Forest has come to life," said Lilly. "But, how…"

"Excuse me!" Charles waddled toward them from the campsite, and as usual early in the morning, he was not in the greatest of moods. "I hope you weren't planning on just leaving me here all alone!"

"Certainly not," said Aidan, laughing. "You're the best scout we have."

"You know that I don't like waking up alone," Charles scolded. "What are you doing just standing about?"

Aidan pointed toward the woods. Charles looked over to the Dead Forest and became silent.

"What do you think of this, Charles?" asked McKenzie. "Isn't it most wondrous?"

"Oh, my, my, my! Quite impressive, oh yes. But, why has the forest come to life? And why now?"

"It's a long story," said Aidan. "I'm not sure if I believe it myself."

As they headed back to the campsite, Aidan told them about his conversation with the Great Sitting Rock the night before. Lilly and McKenzie listened intently, but Charles would have none of it.

"Do you really think that your words did this?" Charles said as he pranced off indignantly. "Why, this part of the country is simply experiencing a late spring. Yes, that's it, a late spring."

"I believe you," said McKenzie. "The trees listened to you, just like the ground did, and just like the river too."

"Aidan," said Lilly, "did you ask Grock about your father?"

"I couldn't. All I could think of was our quest for the elves, and the two of you. I just don't want any harm to come to you or McKenzie."

"I'm not afraid!" stated McKenzie, jumping to her feet.

"Nor am I," said Lilly reassuringly. "Not as long as we are together. Now let's pack up and get moving."

"Lilly is right," said Aidan. "We must get going. Tomorrow is the longest day."

CHAPTER 22

Charles' Gift

Lilly and Aidan were in the final stages of cleaning up the camp area, when Aidan suddenly stopped and looked around.

"Have you seen McKenzie? We'll be off soon, and I'd hate to leave her behind."

"Aidan," Lilly scolded, "you shouldn't joke like that. What if McKenzie heard you?"

"I did hear you!" said McKenzie, walking up from the bank of the river. "But I'm not worried. Aidan knows that if he left me here, there would be no one to protect him!"

Aidan swooped down on McKenzie and whisked her off the ground. "You, protect me?" he teased. McKenzie tried to tickle Aidan but her arms were too short. Aidan put her back down, which proved to be a bad idea.

"Yes, Aidan," she said very proudly as she started tickling him. "After all, I am a warrior, you've said it yourself!"

"Stop!" Aidan cried out in laughter, "not the ribs!"

"All right, then," said McKenzie, out of breath. "Do you promise not to leave me?"

145

"I promise! I promise!" Aidan said as he pulled her close for a hug. "I'll never leave you."

"So, McKenzie, where were you just a few minutes ago?" asked Lilly.

"Oh, I was just over by the river, talking to Bernard. I wanted to thank him for saving us yesterday. He was very polite—he even thanked me for not eating him."

"You found Bernard?" asked Aidan. "You didn't go into the water, did you?"

"No, Aidan, don't worry. I simply stood at the water's edge, and there he was. It was as if he was waiting for me. Oh, I almost forgot, he told me to tell you something very important. He said, 'Tell Aidan he must listen with his heart.'"

Astonished, Aidan said, "Those are the exact words Grock said!"

Just then, there was a splash in the water near the bank. Aidan and the two girls went over to the river, where they saw a bright yellow fish floating at its edge, just below the surface of the water.

"That's Bernard," whispered McKenzie. "I think he's trying to tell us goodbye."

They watched in silence as the brightly colored fish hovered in the water, looking up at them. Then, to their great surprise, it smiled, turned, and swam away.

"Did you see that?" asked McKenzie "He smiled at us!"

"That was a smile?" asked Lilly.

"Yes" laughed Aidan. "That was a fish smile. Now I've seen everything."

IT SMILED, THEN TURNED AND SWAM AWAY

CRRAACCCKKKK!!! Tap! Tap! CRRAACCKK!!!

"What was that?" said a wide-eyed Lilly.

"AAAAAAAAAAAGGGHHHH!!"

"That was Charles," said Aidan. "I'd know that scream anywhere."

From across the clearing, there was a rustling at the edge of the Dead Forest. To the children's surprise, out ran Charles. His eyes were open wide and his pupils were dilated.

Aidan of Oren

"Run for your lives!" he screamed as he ran into Aidan's waiting arms. "There's a monster in the woods!"

"Charles! Calm down," said Aidan. "What were you doing in there all by yourself?"

"I know!" crooned Charles with dismay. "But yesterday I thought I had found a giant pearl! I wanted to give you a gift, just like Lilly and McKenzie did."

"You wanted to give me a monster as a gift?" laughed Aidan. "You're not making sense."

"It's alive!" screeched Charles, "and it's escaping from its horrible egg. We must run away before it eats us!"

"A baby monster!" exclaimed McKenzie. "Let's find it!"

"Wait a minute," cautioned Aidan. "How do you know it's a monster if it's still in an egg?"

Charles was shaking. "The egg is gargantuan. I was trying to move it when a giant claw ripped through the shell, almost taking off my head! A hideous eye was looking at me through the hole in the egg! We must get out of here!"

"I can't believe anything just coming out of an egg could be that dangerous."

"I'm not worried about the egg," agreed Lilly. "I'm worried about what laid it."

"I've just got to see it!" shouted McKenzie, pulling on Aidan's arm. "It's got to be close, let's go!"

Aidan put Charles, who was now only able to make pathetic clicking sounds, on his shoulder. He took McKenzie's hand, and with Lilly close behind the three of them tracked back the way Charles had come. Then they, too, heard the sounds:

CRRAACCCKKKK!!! Tap! Tap! CRRAACCKK!!!

Although a bit alarmed, Aidan pushed onward. As they entered a small clearing, they saw the oddity sitting at the base of a tree.

"Look at that!" squealed McKenzie. "That's fantastic! Do you suppose there's a large baby bird in there?"

"Easy," cautioned Aidan. "Look at the claws poking out the sides of it. I can't tell what it is." He moved closer. There were multiple claws now sticking out of the egg, and there was a crack across the top. Aidan ran his hands over the egg. It was warm. He turned to Lilly, who was standing behind him. "Whatever it is, it wants out!"

The top of the egg cracked open. Aidan whirled around just in time to see two large eyes staring at him through the opening. He froze, not knowing what to do.

"Are you my momma?" came a deep, soft, innocent voice.

Charles snapped out of his trance. "What did he say?"

The top of the egg popped off, revealing the adorably ugly face of the infant beast inside. "Are you my momma?" came the soft, sweet voice again.

"Aidan is most certainly not your momma!" shouted Charles indignantly, his feathers starting to ruffle. "Can someone tell me who taught this baby monster how to talk?"

The ·top ·of ·the ·egg ·popped ·off·

Charles' Gift

"That's a baby dragon!" exclaimed Aidan. "I've heard stories about them. They're ancient creatures endowed with many special gifts. If I remember correctly, they can speak any language, and they are very wise. That must be why humans trusted them to protect the people of Lionsgate."

"A baby dragon!" shouted McKenzie. "Can we keep him?"

Lilly walked up behind Aidan and put her hand on his shoulder. "It doesn't look dangerous. But then, I've never seen anything like it."

All of a sudden the egg rolled over, toppling the creature within it. Aidan reached his arms deep into the egg, freeing the strange beast from its birth chamber.

"I haven't felt anything this slippery since I caught that newt down in Wiley's creek!" he said.

As it sat up, the slime from its former home could be seen sliding down off of its body onto the ground.

"Oh, how revolting!" said Lilly and McKenzie together.

"Aidan!" said Charles sharply, "why don't we just let this *giant* baby whatever be and get on with our journey?"

"No!" cried McKenzie. "We found him. I think we should keep him!"

"He doesn't belong to anyone," said Aidan emphatically.

The infant beast just sat there, looking pathetic. His feet, each with three wiggling toes, were way too large for his body. Compared with his legs, his arms were way too small. His head seemed large and out of proportion, with two small nubs at the top. His wings were small and delicate; certainly not yet developed for flight. But his eyes were large and beautiful, with a hint of sadness.

CHAPTER 23

Damon

cKenzie ran up to the hatchling and threw her arms around it as she said, "I can't believe it! My very own baby dragon!"

"Easy," said Aidan as he pulled McKenzie back. "He does not belong to us. I'm almost afraid to ask where his mother is."

"He doesn't look like a baby dragon to me!" exclaimed Charles. "Besides, even if dragons existed at all, they're supposed to be red. Look at him! He's white!"

Charles had a point. Aidan had always heard that dragons were red. He reached for his pendant and looked at it. This was his only proof of what a dragon should look like, and sure enough, it was a deep, translucent red. Aidan tried to reason with the baby. "Maybe you're really a very large baby bird. I've seen some fairly large white birds before."

"Nooo!" said the little dragon, with a hint of laughter in his voice.

Aidan thought harder. "Maybe, you're one of those duck-billed things."

"Nooo! Noooo!" said the little dragon again. His peculiar voice made him sound almost as if he were laughing. "I'm a baby dragon!" He looked sharply at Aidan. "Momma?"

"I told you!" Charles shouted at the baby dragon, "Aidan is *not your momma*! Do you understand?"

The baby dragon turned his head a bit and looked straight at Charles. "Who's the chicken?"

"I'm not a chicken!" said an enraged Charles. McKenzie started laughing so hard that she fell down.

"I am a regal falcon from the royal family of Wingdom!" he continued, his feathers fully ruffled.

"You talk funny!" said the baby dragon.

At this point, Lilly was laughing as hard as McKenzie. Aidan tried very hard to maintain his composure, but he knew there was a smile creeping across his face. Charles hopped off of Aidan's arm and walked away in a huff.

Aidan knelt down next to the baby dragon and looked in his eyes. "You're not dangerous, are you? There's something you should know," he added. "We are on a journey, and we need to get moving ahead before it gets too late in the day."

The little dragon just sat there, with a very pleasant expression on his face, looking at Aidan.

"All right, then," said Aidan. "We'll be off now. I trust that you'll be alright."

"No!" McKenzie exclaimed. "We can't just leave him here all by himself. He's just a baby."

"Aidan," said Lilly, "if he thinks you're his mother, he obviously doesn't know where his real mother is. That would make him an orphan, wouldn't it?"

"Just like us," added McKenzie softly.

"We wouldn't want to abandon an orphan, now would we?"

"Oh, Lilly," said Aidan. "Honestly, it doesn't really matter what you or I think, because it's not our decision whether or not the baby dragon comes with us." Aidan kneeled down next to the little fellow. "The decision is his."

"Oh, say you want to come with us!" shouted McKenzie to the baby dragon. But he just sat there, staring at Aidan.

"Well, little fellow," said Aidan, "do you want to come with us?"

The baby dragon just looked at Aidan, and very softly said, "Momma."

Aidan shook his head. "He's too big to carry. If he wants to come with us, he can. If not, well, he will just have to look after himself. Whatever the outcome, we need to be on our way."

Aidan turned and headed deeper into the Dead Forest. Lilly and McKenzie lagged behind, glancing back at the baby, but he just sat there, saying "Momma...Momma..." very softly, over and over again.

The girls soon caught up to Aidan and Charles. By then, McKenzie had started to cry. Lilly wrapped her arms around her and told her everything would work out all right.

"We're better off without him," Charles sneered, not even looking back at the girls. Then he put his head down and started shuffling his tiny feet through the twigs on the ground. "Besides, he's probably got some nasty disease or something." His words grew softer. "And, you know, he'd be a very large burden to us all...isn't that...right. I mean...what would one feed a baby...a baby...dragon?"

"What am I hearing?" asked Aidan. "Does Charles really have a soft spot?"

Just then, they heard a strange pitter-pattering noise. Through the trees came the baby dragon—he'd been following them! His walk was quite funny, with his big feet flopping in front of him, but he did seem fully capable of moving about.

"The baby dragon!" shouted Charles and McKenzie together as they ran over to it. Charles wrapped his wings around him, and McKenzie wrapped her arms around them both.

"He wants to come with us!" McKenzie said.

"Ooooof! You're smashing me!" came a muffled cry from Charles.

Aidan was pleased. It did appear that the baby dragon had made the choice to follow them. "If you're going to join us, you'll need a name. I think I'll call you Damon."

"Damon," echoed McKenzie. "I like it!"

Lilly nodded in approval as she said, "Then Damon it shall be."

Damon

CHAPTER 24

Whispering Wind

And then, there were five: Aidan, his two closest friends, his pet falcon, and a baby dragon. They had walked throughout the morning and were getting hungry when they approached a strip of land with no vegetation. Aidan kicked into the dirt, which revealed only small, smooth stones underneath.

Whispering Wind

"How odd," he said as he reached for his pouch. "It looks like there was once a river here, but I didn't see it on the map. I'm sure I would have noticed it before." As he pulled the map from his pouch, Lilly and McKenzie sat on the dry ground to rest.

"I'm hungry!" whimpered Charles as he waddled up to the two girls. "Lilly, might you have something tasty in that basket of yours?"

McKenzie interrupted before Lilly could respond. "Charles, you like berries, don't you?"

"Oh my, yes!" said the excited falcon. "Does Lilly have a few berries for me?"

"No," McKenzie pointed across the way, "but I see some over there!"

This caught Aidan's attention. He put down the map and walked halfway across the dry riverbed. "Are those berries?" he questioned in disbelief. "They're too big!"

"I believe so," said Lilly. "And look, the foliage on the trees on the other side is different than here."

"Maybe we're about to leave the Dead Forest and enter something else," said McKenzie. "Maybe this is a new, mysterious forest that no one's ever seen before." She made claw shapes with her little hands and started reaching for Charles. "It might be scary in there!"

"Aidan!" screamed the terrified falcon.

"Stop teasing, McKenzie. We don't know what's in there," said Aidan. "I'm a little concerned that the map does not show this obvious landmark between what appears to be two different forests. One thing is sure though, we are about to leave the Dead Forest."

"What is this new forest called?" asked Lilly.

"The map says the forest in front of us is called the Woods of Didacus," replied Aidan. "And, the Valley of the Elves is located right in the middle of this forest."

"Oooh…the Woods of Didacus," teased McKenzie, still focusing her attention on Charles.

"Let's take a closer look at that fruit over there," insisted Lilly, who proceeded to walk across the dry riverbed toward the strange looking trees. "We've got to head in this direction anyway."

Aidan and the rest of them followed. As Lilly had pointed out, the foliage was very different from that of the Dead Forest. The plants were bigger, as were the berries that grew wild. Aidan plucked one of the berries from the bushes at the edge of this new forest. It was bright red and as big as an apple, but soft and appealing. When he bit into the strange fruit, a stream of berry juice ran down his chin and onto his shirt.

"It's good!" he exclaimed. "I've never tasted such wonderful fruit in all of my life! I'll bet Grandmama could make a great pie out of these!"

Lilly and McKenzie joined in, trying their best not to stain their own clothing. Charles also found a berry and began eating. All were enjoying the strange and delicious fruit except for Damon, who simply sat back on his haunches.

"Damon, aren't you going to eat anything?" asked Aidan between slurps.

"Maybe dragons don't like fruit," said McKenzie. "Maybe they prefer meat!"

Aidan and Lilly stopped eating.

"I'm sure he's hungry," continued McKenzie. "Hmmmm…" she said, sizing up Charles.

"Don't even *think* it!" quipped the irritated falcon as he waddled over to Aidan. "Please, please pick me up!" he demanded.

The Woods of Didacus presented a delightful change of pace for the sojourning children. Less dense than the Dead Forest, the woods were filled with wonderous plants and trees they had never seen before.

The group headed north without incident, until the light of day began to fade. They stopped in a clearing next to a winding creek to prepare for the night, and lit a small fire.

Aidan of Oren

"The Valley of the Elves is not far from here," said Aidan as he held the map up to the light of the fire. We should easily be there by midday tomorrow, which is the longest day of the year. The prophecy states that this is the only day we can find the elves."

"I want my very own elf!" giggled McKenzie.

"They're not pets," corrected Aidan. "They're people just like you and me, only smaller I think."

"Are you worried that we won't be able to find them?" asked Lilly.

"No, what worries me is that we may find something else."

"The hooded man!" said McKenzie in a loud whisper. Charles, who had not said a word to that point, immediately jumped off Aidan's shoulder and waddled over toward Damon. He put his head back into his tail feathers and tried very hard not to listen.

"Yes, McKenzie, the hooded man," said Aidan soberly. "Let me tell you the story of Gorgon." As the night wore on, Aidan told them the incredible story of a man who was once the Prince of Goth.

"How very sad," said Lilly. "Do you really think Gorgon will try to stop us?"

"I don't know," said Aidan, putting on his bravest face. "But even if he tries to stop us, he will not succeed."

"How can you be so sure?"

"Grandmama told me that the future is what we make it. Destiny has placed us together here and now, but our success is not guaranteed. If we're determined, and work together, we can do anything."

"Are you afraid of seeing Gorgon again?" asked McKenzie.

"Not with you here to protect me!" he laughed.

McKenzie got up and walked over to where Aidan was sitting. She put her little hands on his cheeks, leaned down and kissed him on the nose.

"What was that for?" Aidan asked.

"I've just given you my powers. If that bad man shows up, now you won't be afraid. Not even a little bit!"

"Did the elves tell you to do that?"

"No," she said candidly, folding her little arms in front of her. "I just made it up."

Aidan rubbed the front of his nose thoughtfully. "Thank you, I think. But aren't you going to protect me?"

"No! That big man scares me!"

That made all the children laugh. Aidan was trying very hard not to show his own growing concern. As much as he hoped that they would find the elves before Gorgon found them, somehow he knew that this would not be possible. While Aidan and Lilly discussed what lay ahead of them, McKenzie drifted off to sleep. Lilly quietly worked on her basket as they talked.

Eventually, Aidan asked, "What are you doing?"

"I'm repairing the basket," she said. "It was damaged when the trolls attacked us." Holding it up to the fire-light, she showed Aidan the tear. "With the weave torn like this, the basket has no use. Unless..."

"...Unless you reweave the basket," Aidan finished

her sentence.

"Yes," said Lilly. "Once the weave is restored, the basket will be as good as new."

They continued to talk into the night until Lilly finished her work and went to sleep. Aidan saw that Charles had nestled himself under McKenzie's arm, his newest favorite sleeping spot.

Aidan could not sleep. He got up and walked down to the nearby creek. The wind started to blow in his face as a wave of self-doubt began to get the better of him. He could not stop thinking about the hooded man, the trolls, and Kartha. He had seemed to be so strong, he had to be, for Lilly and McKenzie's sake. But he was not strong now. The thought of facing Gorgon again made his legs weak. The wind suddenly picked up, now coming from all directions, blowing his hair in front of his face.

"I cannot go on!" he shouted to the wind. "My friends are too precious to me to endanger! Let someone else find the elves!"

The wind blew harder.

"I've asked for answers! I've spoken with the Great Sitting Rock, but have come away with only riddles! I am blind to what lies ahead!"

"Therefore, listen not with your ears, but with your heart."

The words of Grock rolled as an echo in the wind, startling him. They were the same words that the mysterious fish Bernard had said to McKenzie. Aidan closed his eyes and shut out all of the thoughts of the day. He even shut out his fears. For this one moment, his mind was clear. Peace fell over him like a warm quilt.

"**Aidan!**"

Startled, he opened his eyes. No one was there. The wind blew in his face even harder. Again, he closed his eyes.

"**Aidan!**" a familiar voice called again.

"Grandmama!" he shouted into the wind. "Is that you? How did you get here?"

"**Why are you sad?**"

"Grandmama, I don't understand...am I dreaming?"

"No my boy, you are not dreaming. But, you are not awake either. You have entered the realm between awake and sleep. It is here that I can talk to you. I've come because your heart has grown weak. You wish to turn back from the destiny that awaits you. Your fear for the safety of your friends has consumed you."

"But, you should have seen what happened…"

"I know about the trolls, Aidan, and I know about Kartha. I was there." Aidan could not believe what he was hearing. "What you fail to see is that no harm came to those you love. It wasn't by chance, my dear. You are their protector. They are safer with you than anywhere else."

"I still don't understand what's happening. I don't understand you. Help me, Grandmama."

"You are learning about yourself, my child. You have abilities that you cannot yet comprehend, but you will in time."

"Is that why I was chosen to free the guardians?"

"Yes, and much more. Your quest will heal the land and bring peace back to the people. It has already begun, the Dead Forest is dead no longer."

"I did that?"

"Yes, Aidan. Tomorrow you will restore something else, something very precious."

"What do you mean, Grandmama?" I don't understand. I'm worried that I'm not prepared for what will happen tomorrow."

Whispering Wind

"Oh, but you are prepared. This very evening, your two companions have given you everything you need to face tomorrow."

"But…"

"Open your eyes my child. Open your eyes and you will understand."

Aidan opened his eyes. There on a rock was the answer to his question. Although he could not believe what he was seeing, Aidan knew what he had to do.

CHAPTER 25

McKenzie's Song

During the night, a rolling fog blanketed the woods. Lilly was awakened by the sound of soggy footsteps. She sat up just in time to see Aidan plop down on the ground across from the ashes of last night's fire.

"You're all wet!" she exclaimed.

"You'll never guess what I found!" said Aidan, trying to catch his breath. "You see, last night I was talking to…"

"Wait! Where's McKenzie?" Lilly was frantic. "She's not here!"

"Shhh!" Aidan held his finger in front of his lips. "Listen…" A soft, small voice could be heard in the distance. "Do you hear her?"

Lilly listened for a moment as a broad grin broke across her face. "McKenzie's singing!" she whispered. "I try so hard to get her to sing with me while we work, but she's just too shy!"

"That's funny!" laughed Aidan. "I can't believe McKenzie could be shy about anything!"

"Only her singing, but doesn't she have the sweetest little voice?"

Aidan closed his eyes. "She sings like an angel."

There was a shuffling under McKenzie's blanket, and then Charles stuck his head out. "What's all the racket?" he asked.

"Shhh!" Aidan scolded. "McKenzie's singing, and we're trying to enjoy it." Charles ducked back under the blanket, mumbling something about needing more sleep. Aidan noticed that Damon was also awake. He seemed to be listening to McKenzie off in the distance and, for the first time, appeared happy.

"Let's go see where she is," Aidan said. "But we should be very quiet so as not to interrupt her."

"I like singing," said Damon, as he quietly pitter-pattered his way toward the direction of McKenzie's voice. Aidan helped Lilly up, and together they followed the little dragon down the path. They rounded a very large tree, and were greeted by the most beautiful sight.

McKenzie had found a strand tied between two giant flowers. With her arms held out to each side, McKenzie balanced herself three feet off the ground. She was singing a most beautiful song.

"Isn't that lovely?" asked Lilly, who stood behind the tree, out of sight from McKenzie. "This is such a perfect moment."

"Doesn't she have great balance?" asked Aidan. "You know, I'm the one who taught her how to walk on narrow logs."

"Look at those huge flowers! I wonder where she got that rope?"

"Don't be silly," said Aidan. "There's no rope out

Aidan of Oren

Doesn't She have a great Balance? asked Aidan

here, and those flowers… Wait! If the flowers are that large, what else could be large out here?" With a chill running down his spine, Aidan immediately ran over to McKenzie.

"What are you doing here?" she said, startled.

Aidan touched the rope McKenzie was balancing on, and yanked his hand back in horror.

"This isn't a rope, McKenzie!" he said as he put her on his shoulders. "It's sticky! It feels like the kind of strand a spider might make!"

"Aidan," said Lilly, now starting to panic, "how large of a spider would it take to make a strand like that?"

A loud rumbling sound startled the children. "I'm hungry," said Damon as he tugged on Aidan's pants.

There's no time for that!" said Aidan. With McKenzie still on his shoulders, he hurried back toward camp. Lilly and Damon were not far behind.

"We should pack our things and continue to the northwest," said Aidan, obviously worried.

"Where's Charles?" asked Mckenzie.

"He was sleeping under the blanket when we left," said Lilly, as she ran her hands through the bedding, "but he's not here now!" The falcon was nowhere to be found. Suddenly, Damon bounded back down the path from which they had just come.

"Damon! No!" shouted Aidan. "We mustn't split up!" But Damon was gone.

"We have to wait here until they come back," said Lilly. "We can't risk getting split up any more than we already are." McKenzie kept calling for Damon and

Charles, but there was no answer.

"We've got to do something," said Aidan. "They're both helpless out there…"

A shriek sliced through the forest.

"AAAAAAAAAAAGGGHHHH!!"

"I've heard that scream before," said Aidan. "It's Charles!" Before he could say another word, they heard something else. It sounded like a low, deep breath, but it was very loud. It echoed eerily through the Dead Forest. Then, there was silence. The children were helplessly looking at each other, wondering what to do next, when Charles came running frantically up the path, his eyes open wide. "The spi…huge…spi…" was all he could say.

"What happened?" asked Aidan as he ran over and picked up his falcon.

"I…I was caught in something…very sticky…"

"Go on, Charles. You're safe, now."

"This horribly large spider…no, it was more of a monster…it was coming for me…and…I couldn't move!" Charles started to shake.

Aidan put his hand over Charles' head and tucked him close to his chest. "Go on, old friend. Tell us what happened."

"Alright. Well…the beast had backed me into a corner. He was going to eat me when Damon came out of nowhere! He…he…he approached the eight-legged monster with no fear at all! Then…our little friend breathed fire out of his mouth and burned it alive!"

"I can't believe it! He's too young for that, isn't he?"

"How would we know?" asked McKenzie. "We've never had a pet dragon before."

"That's not all!" Charles butted in. "After charbroiling the monster…Damon…he…"

"What did he do, Charles?" asked Aidan.

"He…he…oh, you don't want to know!"

Just then Damon pitter-pattered his way into the clearing. He looked up at his friends, put his hand over his mouth, and burped mightily.

"Oh, how disgusting!" exclaimed Lilly.

"You ate the monster!" yelled McKenzie as she went over and hugged Damon. "And, you saved Charles. Aren't you wonderful!"

"Oh, he's wonderful alright," said Aidan. "A baby dragon that eats monsters. Now, that's what I call a good traveling companion." He unrolled the map and began to plot their course when he noticed Damon walking across the campsite, toward the forest.

"Now where are you going?" asked Aidan. "Are you still hungry?"

"Momma?" was all that the little dragon said as he continued away. And then, he started cooing softly.

Aidan's heart raced. Had Damon found his mother? Were they now in dreadful danger? Aidan gathered Lilly and McKenzie closer to him.

Then, suddenly, Damon stopped at Aidan's bedding. The children's hearts melted as they watched the little dragon gently reach down and pick up Aidan's necklace and hold it to his chest. With his head sorrowfully pointed downward he said, "Momma, Momma."

Aidan of Oren

The dragon scale! He had never thought Aidan was his mother; it was the pendant that drew him.

"I'm sorry, Damon" said Aidan, as the children walked up toward him. "Did that scale come from your mother?"

The little dragon looked up at Aidan and nodded.

Aidan knelt down and gave his best attempt at a smile. "You can keep that," he said, with his voice trembling. "I believe it belongs to you."

Damon continued to clutch the necklace. Aidan wondered what could be going through his infant brain. Then, the little dragon put the necklace over Aidan's head as he quietly said, "Friends."

Aidan looked at Lilly and McKenzie and then back to Damon as he said, "Yes indeed, Damon, we are friends."

Aidan ran his hand down the center of Damon's back, where he found spines running from the top of his head down to his little pointed tail. They were hard, and cool to the touch. Looking at him, his back and chest areas appeared soft. However, Aidan was amazed to find out that this white exterior was actually crystal-like to the touch, almost like armor. How could something so hard look so soft? What marvelous creatures these dragons must be.

'Friends,' he thought to himself. 'No, little prince, I believe that we will be much more than friends.'

CHAPTER 26

Return of Gorgon

oon they had everything packed up and were ready to continue their journey. They walked north through the Woods of Didacus. The woods seemed to be changing with every step as the wondrous, oversized plants and trees were replaced with moss-filled trees boasting giant roots. They pushed along until they could go forward no longer. They had arrived at a large swamp.

"We're going to have to choose another way," said Aidan, pulling out his map. "We certainly can't walk through that swamp. There's no telling how deep the water is or what creatures might be lurking in there. If we head east and follow this path around, we would be able to avoid this area."

"Won't that take us out of our way?" asked Lilly. "This is the day that we're to find the elves, isn't it?"

"It's alright!" shouted McKenzie from behind. "Let's go straight! I'm not afraid of anything lurking in there!"

"I think Aidan has a good point," said Charles. "Safety first, you know."

"Oh, Charles, you're just scared!" said McKenzie.

"Of course I'm scared! You weren't the one being attacked by that multi-legged monster!"

"Aidan," Lilly started, "We don't have much time to..."

"No, I've made my decision," he interrupted. "We will use the eastern path and go around. I don't want to put us in any more danger. We'll just have to move quickly."

Aidan chose a path that led them closer to the hills in the east, away from the swamp. The path looked longer, but Aidan could see no other way.

Morning soon turned into afternoon as the sun raced across the sky. Aidan began to worry that he had underestimated the time it would take to use this path. They stopped at a small waterfall where they were able to refresh themselves, but quickly moved on in an attempt to make up precious time. Both Aidan and Lilly tried to find things to talk about, hoping to ease the tension that was building with each step. But it was of no use. There was only one thing on their minds—how much longer would it be until they arrived in the Valley of the Elves?

Aidan breathed a heavy sigh. "The sun will soon be setting. I'm not quite sure how much farther we have to go. But, I know that we're headed in the right direction."

"We'd be a lot farther along if those trolls hadn't attacked us the other day," said Lilly.

"And, even further if that swamp hadn't forced us to take the long way around," added Aidan.

"Aren't hills supposed to go up and down, up and

down?" asked McKenzie. "We've been traveling down for quite a while now without going up. Isn't that a bit strange?"

With everything else on his mind, Aidan hadn't noticed. But, she was right. They had been traveling downward for a very long time. He pulled the map out of his pouch and studied it. "We had to travel east in order to avoid the swamp," he said, trying his best to sound confident, "and now, we're traveling northwest. We should be headed directly for the Valley of the Elves." Aidan rolled up the map and surveyed the land in front of them. "The entrance to the valley should be over there."

Charles popped his head up. "What valley? Surely not the valley of the monsters?"

"There's no such thing as the valley of the monsters," laughed Aidan, "at least, not that I'm aware of. Anyway, now you have a baby dragon to protect you."

Suddenly, a voice rang out just in front of them. "Your dragon cannot protect you from me!"

"*It is* the valley of the monsters!" shrieked Charles. "I knew it... I just knew it!"

The group stopped suddenly.

"Who said that?" asked Aidan nervously.

"Come closer, Aidan of Oren! Come and watch as your destiny comes to an end!"

◘

CHAPTER 27

So Shall It Be

Lilly and McKenzie, hide quickly!" said Aidan. "Damon and Charles will come with me." The girls immediately did as he said.

"No, no, no!" said Charles. It didn't matter, he was not given a choice. Aidan led them up the path and past a line of trees. The hooded man was there, standing at the spot where the path forked out in two separate directions. Behind him were the blackest clouds that Aidan had ever seen. Lightning was shooting out of them toward the earth in a most frightening display of power.

"I don't think so!" said Charles as he leaped to the ground. He ran and stood behind Damon, who did not seem afraid at all.

"Gorgon!" gasped Aidan.

"I told you that we would meet again!" His voice resonated through the forest as he pointed to the setting sun. "And, as you can see, you have failed! I have broken the prophecy!"

"You?" asked Aidan bravely. "What have you done to break the prophecy?"

"I've heard all about you, Aidan of Oren," gloated

Gorgon. "I knew of the prophecy, and I knew you would be coming in search of the elves. I have wandered this forest for decades and know the area better than any creature alive! I knew that if I could stall you long enough, you would never find the elves in time!"

"How did you stall me?"

"Remember the little band of trolls in the Northern Forest? They are friends of mine…well, they *were* friends of mine!" Gorgon laughed hideously. "You managed to elude Kartha, and for some reason I can't find my pet spider. Regardless, they all succeeded by slowing you down."

"Run, Aidan!" yelled McKenzie from back in the trees. "Run up the trail! Maybe you can still find the elves!"

"Yes, run!" laughed Gorgon. "Pick one of these paths and run! But you had better hope your decision is the right one!"

Lilly, who was also standing back behind the tree line, peeked up to see that the sun had almost completely set. "Aidan, you must make a decision quickly!"

"I stand before the great child of Oren!" mocked Gorgon. "I was told this would be a most difficult task. Why, you don't even know who you are!" Again, his evil laughter thundered through the woods.

Damon moved forward and stood beside Aidan.

"What are you doing?!" shrieked Charles, trying his best to stay right behind the little dragon. "Stop moving!"

Aidan put his hand out and stopped Damon. "This

is not your fight, my friend. Step back and stay with Lilly and McKenzie. See that no harm comes to them." The little dragon nodded and moved back with the two girls. Charles waddled close behind.

"Oh, isn't that touching?" hissed Gorgon. "You choose to save your friends, but you cannot even save yourself." He looked to the western sky, and then back at Aidan. "The sun has set," he said triumphantly. "It is over!"

Aidan could hear Lilly and McKenzie softly sobbing behind him. He wanted to comfort them, but he had something much more important to do. He walked up to the feet of Gorgon and knelt down.

"What are you doing?" said Gorgon, taking a step back.

"I am bowing to a prince. Is this not appropriate?"

"Stop it! I am a prince no more! That was so long ago!" The thunder and lightning in the clouds behind Gorgon intensified.

"Royal blood runs through your veins," said Aidan, this time a little louder. "A youthful mistake. Shunned by your own. Still, the son of a king you are. I bring a gift to the prince of Goth."

"A gift?" asked Gorgon, his voice softening. Aidan reached into his pouch and pulled out something… something that shook Gorgon's very soul. "An imp!" he gasped.

"You've paid such a heavy price," said Aidan as he placed the hideous little creature with the pale blue eyes into the trembling hands of his enemy.

Aidan of Oren

"You've PAID SUCH A HEAVY PRICE" SAID AIDAN

So Shall It Be

The little creature immediately looked into Gorgon's eyes and said:

"What do you see when you look at me?"

A voice erupted out of the blackness. "No! I Forbid it!"

Gorgon did not respond. With one massive hand holding the imp, Gorgon pulled away his hood with the other, clearly revealing his twisted face and wretched countenance. His gaze was locked with that of the imp. "I see a lonely man," he said softly. "I see a heart, once hardened, now broken. I see a prince." The wind started blowing violently. Lightning started striking the earth behind Gorgon, whose attention turned to Aidan.

Then, the little imp in Gorgon's hand spoke. **"So shall it be. So shall it be."**

"You fool!" came a voice from the black sky above. "He has defeated you!"

"No!" shouted Gorgon as he turned to face the menacing sky. "He has saved me!" His words seemed to echo on forever. The lightning stopped and the black clouds dispersed, revealing the first twinkling stars of the night. All was silent.

Gorgon walked over to the nearby stream where he knelt down to set the little imp free. The moon shone brightly on the water. Nervously, he glanced down and gasped as he saw his reflection in the river. His large frame shuddered as he proceeded to sob uncontrollably. "So many years wasted. So many that I've hurt."

Aidan approached Gorgon, but didn't know what to say. The sobbing stopped, and the tall hooded man stood to his feet. He slowly turned around. "Aidan of Oren," he said, "it is a pleasure to meet you. I am Gorgon, Prince of Goth."

So MANY YEARS, WASTED...

CHAPTER 28

The Prince of Goth

Your face!" Aidan was startled to see a tall, handsome man standing in front of him.

"Thank you, my friend," said Gorgon, as he shook Aidan's hand. "You have broken the curse that I've borne for a lifetime. Many years ago, I wish I could have shown the compassion that you have shown me today. I owe you my life. How did you know about me?"

"I've heard stories…" Aidan said.

"But you showed no fear. How is that possible?"

Aidan glanced over to the clearing and saw McKenzie. "I was given the courage of a warrior," he said proudly.

The Prince of Goth shook his head. "You knew about the prophecy. Why didn't you choose a path? Why didn't you try?"

"Oh, but I did choose a path. That path was you." Lilly and McKenzie had now worked up enough courage to come out and stand beside Aidan. Damon followed, with a trembling Charles close behind. Gorgon was speechless as Aidan continued. "You said yourself that you know this forest better than anyone alive. I think you know how to find the elves."

"I do," replied Gorgon. "But how did you know that I would help you?"

"Because, I helped restore you. All we had to do was reweave the basket." Aidan winked at Lilly. "What happened to you long ago was a tragedy, but it has brought you to us so that you can now help us. The path is yours to choose, not mine."

"That would mean that I have not lived my life in vain," the Prince said, wiping away a tear.

"Of course not."

The great prince knelt down beside Aidan and said, "Tell me, my friend, how can I help you?"

"Please," said Aidan as he helped the prince back to his feet, "show us how to find the elves."

"I see great confidence in you, Aidan. Your friends have chosen well. Follow me." Gorgon, rather than choosing the left or right path, chose to go directly between them into the thick of the woods.

Aidan and the others quickly followed.

"Reweave the basket?" Lilly asked as she caught up with Aidan. "I remember talking to you about that, but I can't remember why."

"I do," Aidan chuckled. "You're wiser than you think!"

"But where did you get the imp?"

"That's a bit harder to explain," said Aidan. "Last night, Grandmama spoke to me in the wind. She told me that you and McKenzie had already helped me and that when I opened my eyes I would understand."

"So, I opened my eyes and saw a tiny imp. It was sitting on a rock, looking at its reflection in the water. I remembered the story told by Helfin and approached it carefully. It asked me the same question that it asked Gorgon, but I was careful not to say anything. When the little creature saw that I was not going to answer, it ran away. It took me all night to catch it!"

"That explains your wet clothes!"

Aidan laughed. "Yes, and lucky for me, imps sleep during the day. Had he been awake, I would have had a hard time explaining what was hopping around in my pouch!"

"Aidan!" cried Charles. "Damon's tail is kicking me all over the forest. Please put me on your shoulder!"

"What's the bird's name?" asked Gorgon as they continued walking.

"Oh," said McKenzie, "that's just Charles. He complains a lot, doesn't he?"

"He certainly seems to. Can he fly?"

"I could if I wanted to!" interrupted Charles. "Just where are we going? We seem to be in the middle of nowhere!"

"Your bird is quite smart," said Gorgon as he stopped walking. "We're here in the middle of nowhere. Where else would you expect to find the elves?"

"There's nothing here but an old tree stump!" crooned Charles. "Why are we trusting this man?"

"The old tree stump your feathered friend refers to is very special. This was the oldest tree in the entire country, the first ever planted. That was many years ago."

"Gorgon," asked Aidan excitedly, "are you saying that this…?"

"Yes," replied Gorgon, "this is the entrance to the Valley of the Elves."

"I don't understand," said Lilly.

Aidan ventured a guess. "If no one has ever seen the elves, then they must not live where people do, right?"

A huge grin spread across McKenzie's face.

"And, if I really did hear the voices of elves echoing from my well, then they must live underground!"

"Mmm, not exactly," said McKenzie, her grin fading.

"Oh, this is good!" groaned Charles. "Little people that live underground, and the only way to get to them is through an old tree stump. I can't stand it!"

"Aidan," cautioned Gorgon. "I don't mean to dampen your hopes, but aren't we a little late?"

"I don't think so. I thought of something last night as I tried to go to sleep. Looking up at the sky, I noticed the beautiful, bright, moon. Just like we have tonight." Everyone looked up to the sky. "Tell me, where does the moon get its light?"

"From the sun!" said Gorgon. "It's still shining down on us from the moon!"

"That's what I'm counting on," said Aidan. "The day is not over! Now, one last problem, how do we get in?"

"Knock with your heart," said McKenzie softly. "You have to knock with your heart."

Aidan and Gorgon, having no idea what McKenzie was saying, just shrugged their shoulders.

Gorgon knelt down by McKenzie and held her little hands. "Alright, my little angel, how does one knock with his heart?"

"By singing," she said matter-of-factly. "I'll show you." She turned toward the massive tree stump, and started singing in the most beautiful voice any of them had ever heard. The words of her song seemed spell-binding; the music was haunting. Damon softly cooed along, almost as if he was singing with her.

"Look!" said Lilly. "The stump is changing!"

Indeed, it was changing. A little red door appeared on the side of the majestic stump.

McKenzie stopped singing. All were silent as the little red door slowly opened, revealing a tiny elf with golden hair and a curious smile.

"Oh, you've got to be kidding me…" said Charles, just before Aidan grabbed his beak.

CHAPTER 29

Sebastian Fry

"Τhis is where I say goodbye," said Gorgon. "I must return to my kingdom."

"Do you have to leave so soon?" asked Aidan. "We've just found the elves!"

"My father is very old and not in good health. It is my hope that he will be able to lay his eyes upon me before he dies."

"I'm sorry. I hope you see your father soon."

Gorgon put his large right hand on Aidan's shoulder. "I hope you see your father soon, as well. You are very much like him."

"Did you know my father?"

"Yes, Aidan. We were friends, although sometimes I wonder why he befriended me. I was always the impetuous one, acting before I thought things through. But your father, he was cautious and took nothing for granted. Like you, he was strong yet compassionate. He's the best of all men."

"Where can I find him?"

"Aidan, the fact that you're here means he has already found *you*. Somehow, he has awakened your spirit."

Aidan thought back to his dream, and grabbed the prince by the arm. "Gorgon! Do you know anything about a white horse with wings?"

"You speak of Camar, your father's horse. There is no other horse like that in the entire world. How did you know?"

Suddenly, it all made sense. The dream he had a few days ago was his father's way of waking him up. Aidan's soul soared within him as the hope that he would soon see his father seemed to be more than just hope. *It would happen!*

"If you were really a friend of Aidan's father," asked McKenzie, "why did you try and hurt him when we were in the market?"

The Prince of Goth replied, "I was sent to find him, not to hurt him." The tall prince gathered the three children close to him. "I hope you can forgive me for serving the Lord of Dunjon. My heart was not my own."

McKenzie reached up and hugged him tightly and whispered in his ear: "Just promise never to do it again."

"I promise," he said as he stood to leave.

"The Lord of Dunjon," said Aidan, "was that the voice we heard in the black sky?"

"Yes," said Gorgon soberly. "The Lord of Dunjon is not happy about your success. Beware of him, he is much stronger than you can possibly imagine."

"Thank you," said Aidan. "I will take your words to heart."

"I think the elf is telling us to follow him!" said Lilly. Sure enough, the tiny elf was calling them toward the little red door. Gorgon waved goodbye to all and disappeared into the forest.

"Well," said Aidan as he put his arms around Lilly and McKenzie, "are you ready for a new adventure?"

"I'm not going in there!" said Charles indignantly. "I don't like small places!"

"It's not small!" gleamed McKenzie. "I've heard the elves speak of their home. It's as big in there as it is out here!"

Lilly was more cautious. "Are we really going down there?" The tiny elf with the curious little smile walked up and took Lilly's hand. "Look! I think he's trying to tell me it's alright!"

"Can we take Damon with us?" asked Aidan.

The little elf nodded in approval.

"What about me?" screamed Charles. "I've gotten you this far, are you just going to abandon me?"

Aidan knelt down beside the curious little creature that stood only slightly higher than his waist. "What is your name?"

Aidan of Oren

The little elf responded with a rhyme:

**"The leader of the elves, am I,
My proper name is Sebastian Fry.
So now I ask, step through the tree
For this is where you're meant to be."**

"Hello Sebastian," said Aidan. "Pleased to meet you. I hear that there is much you can teach us." The little elf nodded in agreement.

"Well then," Aidan paused and took a deep breath, "we look forward to learning about you, and about the ancient ways."

Sebastian led each of them, one by one, with Charles complaining all the while, through the little red door.

CHAPTER 30

World Within a World

Although the little red door in the old tree stump appeared to be very small, the children experienced no difficulty as they bent down and passed through. To their great surprise, they came out immediately from another tree stump that looked mysteriously like the one that they had just entered. Everything around them looked exactly the same.

Aidan placed his hand gently on Sebastian Fry's little shoulder. "What happened? It seems that we haven't gone anywhere at all."

"Of course we have!" said McKenzie. "We're in their world now."

"I don't think so," mocked Charles. "We simply passed through the tree. I think our little friend here is playing games with us."

"I might just have to agree with Charles, for once," said Aidan, as he rubbed his hand up against the bark of the old tree stump. "This is the same stump and doorway we just entered. We haven't had time to go anywhere. Look, the line of trees is the same, there's Zorn Mountain and...what?!?"

Aidan of Oren

Welcome to Our Home, My Friend

Aidan gasped. He could not believe his eyes. "Two mountains!"

Sebastian Fry pointed toward the twin mountains.

**"Welcome to our home, my friend.
It's not of where, but when,
An age when mountains touched the sky
Together once again."**

World Within a World

Aidan did not know what to say, but McKenzie did. "When can we see your village?" she asked, beaming with excitement. "Is it far from here?"

Lilly rubbed her eyes. She was trying her best to stay attentive, but it had been a long day. Even Aidan could not stop the yawn slowly spreading across his face. Sebastian Fry took Aidan's hand and started walking north.

**"We knew you would be tired,
On this, the longest day.
We have prepared a fire, and more.
Please come, and walk this way."**

The little elf led the children to the side of a ridge, where they found a small, unusual house built between two large oak trees. The walls around the outside of the house were formed with crooked, uneven stones, and the roof was covered with thatched straw held together by long sticks. In front of the house, a large fire had been carefully built, lending light to reveal a most amazing sight. Near the fire, a table had been prepared. The wooden table was perfectly round with a large base. On top of the table was more food than Aidan had ever seen. Fruit of all kinds was surrounded by curiously round loaves of bread. Sweets and cheeses were piled high—more than they could eat in a day. Sebastian Fry led them to three small chairs in front of the table and bid the children to seat themselves. Lilly and McKenzie sat quickly, but Aidan did not. His sense of good manners would not allow it.

"Sebastian," he said, "there's more food here than the

Aidan of Oren

three of us can possibly eat, won't you join us?"

The little elf with the curious smile pointed to Aidan's chair.

> **"The table is to welcome you,**
> **The food, to keep you strong.**
> **I am just your humble host,**
> **To join you would be wrong."**

Sebastian Fry turned toward the little stone house and clapped his hands three times.

> **"Walter! Sprite! Frederick!**
> **Come out and meet our friends.**
> **Bring the gifts that you've prepared,**
> **The cotton and the blends;**
> **Take care to keep them all complete,**
> **Fold them twice, in two's.**
> **Hurry, now, the night is short**
> **And don't forget the shoes."**

The shuffling of little feet preceded a most charming sight. Three little elves, each carrying a set of clothing, came scurrying out of the little stone house and stood before the children.

The smallest of the elves moved forward first. He presented his colorful bundle to McKenzie, who immediately jumped from her chair to hug the little elf. As she picked him up, she heard a little "oof!"

"Oh, I'm so sorry!" she said. "I didn't mean to hurt you." The little elf's lips moved, but no sound came out. McKenzie put her ear close to his little mouth and grinned as she heard what the little elf had to say.

The·Smallest·of·the·Elves·Moved·Forward·First

"His name is Frederick!" she exclaimed as she unfolded his gift to her.

"This is a dress!" McKenzie put Frederick down and held the dress up in front of her. "Look, it's my size!"

In same fashion, the little elf named Walter presented his gift to Lilly, who echoed McKenzie's enthusiasm.

Then, the third little elf, Sprite, presented her gift to Aidan. She was remarkably pretty, and very different from the others. Her eyes were larger, and her pointed ears markedly smaller than the others.

"Thank you," Aidan said as he took the gift from her small hands.He held the clothing up in the light of the fire, pleasantly surprised at what he found. "Remarkable! It's my size, too!" He turned to Sebastian Fry, who seemed to be very happy with the way things were turning out. "How did you know?"

> "**Knowledge comes from learning,**
> **Learning comes with time.**
> **Ancient words were spoken**
> **With the sounding of the chime**
> **Spoken of three children**
> **In meanings that were clear,**
> **And so we've known for ages**
> **Today you would be here.**"

Aidan scratched his head and gazed over at Lilly and McKenzie. They all started laughing. Partly because they were very tired, and partly because they had no idea what Sebastian Fry was talking about.

The leader of the elves led Aidan back to his seat at the table. Lilly and McKenzie also took their seats, and the children feasted as they never had before.

Charles, who had been pleasantly quiet that evening, particularly liked the grapes that fell from the table. But, as calm as he appeared to be, he was careful not to stray very far from the side of Damon, who seemed to prefer the bread.

"Sebastian," said Aidan between bites, "so this is where you live? Where are all of the other elves?"

Aidan of Oren

Sebastian Fry shook his head from side to side.

> "Our village is not far from here,
> The other elves are there.
> When morning comes we'll take a walk,
> We'll have more time to spare."

"No!" shouted McKenzie as she rubbed here eyes. "I want to see the elf village tonight!"

Aidan reached over and hugged his little warrior friend. "If Sebastian Fry says tomorrow, then it will have to be tomorrow. We are their guests."

McKenzie nodded, still rubbing her tired eyes.

Sebastian Fry sent Walter, Sprite, and Frederick home, then bid Aidan and the children to follow him inside the little stone house. The doorway was so low that Aidan and Lilly had to duck down as they entered. Inside, they found three small beds. Sebastian Fry stepped to the back of the little building and stood next to the lone window. He pointed toward the bright moon shining in.

> "The moon is bright, the air is right,
> This stage, prepared for years.
> The crickets' sound heard all around
> Forms music in our ears.
> So as we start this symphony,
> I leave you with a bow.
> The ancient seal awaits, but,
> Rest yourselves for now."

Before any of the children could say a word, Sebastian Fry whisked out of the little building.

World Within a World

Aidan, who was very tired at this point, sat down on one of the little beds. Damon quickly shuffled his way to the foot of Aidan's bed and hunched down as if ready to retire for the night. Charles was close behind, and getting irritated.

"Must you always follow Aidan around like that?" he grimaced.

Aidan let out a soft laugh as he laid back and rested his head on the curious little pillow provided. "What a comfortable bed!" he exclaimed. "It's a little small, but it feels just like my bed at home!"

"Mine does, too!" said Lilly with delight. "It almost feels like we're nestling down in our very own beds!" Then she started laughing. "What if this was all just a dream? What if..."

"Don't joke like that!" said McKenzie. "I don't want to wake up back at the orphanage. I want to wake up to a brand new world!"

The three children bedded down and prepared themselves for a well-deserved rest. Lilly fell asleep first, then McKenzie with Charles tucked under her arm. Damon was snoring softly at the foot of Aidan's bed, but Aidan didn't notice. He lay back in his bed, lost in thought as he stared out through the lone window. He could see the twin mountains, standing side by side, and he wondered what it meant. His thoughts raced through the events of the day. Gorgon, the imp, passing through the tree stump. It all seemed so far away now. All seemed peaceful, and his eyes grew heavy as the night wore on.

"AWAKE! AWAKE!" he sat straight up in bed. He had heard those words before. Aidan bounded out through the little door. It was still dark and fog had consumed the land. He heard something walking toward him and stepped back. Through the haze, he could see that the great white horse with wings had returned and was approaching him.

"Camar?" Aidan asked, "Is that your name?" The muscular horse stopped in front of him and started grazing peacefully. "Camar, where's my father?"

The great beast raised its head and tilted it to one side, as if he was studying Aidan. Then, it turned its head and looked back into the darkness from whence it came.

World Within a World

"Am I dreaming?" asked Aidan.

A voice boomed from the woods. **"As a boy you dreamed."**

Aidan awoke with a start. Beads of sweat had formed on his brow. All was silent. His friends lay sleeping peacefully in their beds. "No!" he shouted, running outside. There was no fog, and to his great disappointment, there was no horse. He searched the area all around the little house, but in vain. They were alone. Aidan slowly walked back inside and returned to his bed. He wondered at the big voice, knowing that it was the same voice that awoke him a few days earlier.

Aidan felt a gentle breeze coming in through the window. He turned toward the breeze, which felt good on his face. "I will find you," he said into the breeze. As he again started drifting off to sleep, he repeated over and over, "I will find you, I will..."

Outside, all was at peace. In his search through the woods, had Aidan ventured just a little farther to the top of the crest, he would have seen a most magnificent sight. Thousands of tiny lights dotted the landscape, which opened into a great valley. Thousands of tiny elf houses, all lit by candlelight, surrounded the great elf city at the center of the valley.

Inside all of the tiny houses, the elves, like the children, were waiting with great anticipation for the new day. A great celebration had been prepared, a celebration for the children long foretold. A celebration for the ages.

Aidan of Oren

But that's another story.